MY HUSBAND'S WIFE

A totally addictive psychological thriller
with a shocking twist

ANYA MORA

Originally published as
The Wife Lie

Revised edition 2023
Joffe Books, London
www.joffebooks.com

First published in Great Britain in 2020 as *The Wife Lie*

This paperback edition was first published
in Great Britain in 2023

Cover art by Nick Castle

ISBN: 978-1-83526-050-0

CHAPTER 1

I've always been resourceful, even before kids. My life requires it.

"Are they ready?" Clementine asks, jumping up and down.

"Just hang on a sec, Tiny." I slap the final piece of duct tape on the hem of her jeans and then fold down the cuff. "There. Now they're tailor-made for you."

After handing them over to Clementine, I watch her pull the bright pink second-hand pants on her four-year-old frame. Her smile is contagious. I knew she'd love them the moment I saw the pants on the rack at the thrift store, two sizes too big.

"They're perfect, Mama." She squeezes my neck tight and kisses my cheek, making me laugh.

I tickle her until she's rolling on the floor in a heap of giggles. "Now your grandma won't fuss about your pants dragging past your feet." I grab the tape and scissors and stand up from her bedroom floor. "Now where's your brother? We have to get going. My shift starts in a half hour."

"Benny!" Tiny shouts, bounding out of her pink-and-purple bedroom, looking for her twin brother.

I follow after her down the single hallway of our three-bedroom rambler, toward the kitchen. Built in the

1950s, it's solid and simple, and I still thank my lucky stars we were able to find this rental last year.

"We can't afford this," I'd said, looking back at Ledger, who had brought me here.

"I got a raise, baby," he said, eyes as green as pine trees. He pulled me into his arms and he kissed me hard and I laughed. Three whole bedrooms. A back yard. A washing machine. A dryer. No more pockets full of quarters.

The smile is still on my face. Now, I shove the mending supplies in the kitchen junk drawer, and I look up to see Benny perched on a stool at the table. He's forgotten his Crunchios and is instead busy working on the Lego set he just earned for not having any nighttime accidents for a week. We may be pinching pennies, but incentives work. And I'm good at stashing my tips until I've saved the cash I need for my kids.

"Hey, buddy, we gotta go." I look at the clock on the microwave. "We're already late."

He takes his last few bites of cereal, pointing to his creation. "Can I bring it with me?" He turns, seeing me with a quart-sized plastic baggie, and he smiles. "Thanks, Mama."

I turn off the coffee pot and toss my phone into my purse, pulling my unruly curls into a hair-tie as I walk to the front door. Tiny's bright pink legs race past me, Benny following close behind. It's going to be a hot day, but she insisted on those pants. I couldn't resist her pleas. And why would I? Life is hard enough; no reason to deny a little girl a simple pleasure.

The moment I start the car, I groan, calculating the cost of a much-needed tank. I make sure the kids are buckled into their booster seats before I back the minivan out the driveway. Bethany is in her yard, filling up the kiddie pool, her six-month-old, Neva, in her arms, and Thomas, her three-year-old, running around in circles with their dog. She waves at me and I roll down the window.

"Hey, Penny, heading to work?" she asks.

I nod. "Yeah, my mom's watching the kids."

"I can always help." Neva starts crying, and Bethany bounces her on her hip.

I smile, knowing my closest friend has her hands full enough as it is. "My mom likes having the kids around."

"Ledger home soon?"

"Tonight." Smirking, I add, "Which means I should probably clean up a bit."

Bethany laughs. "Hey, we need a wine night soon. Word on the street is Joanne and Marty split up. I've got too much gossip and no one to spill it with."

"I'm in," I say, waving goodbye. I keep the window down. It's only nine in the morning, but it's mid-August in western Washington, and the heat is here to stay for the next month at least. Punching on the radio with my index finger, I pick a morning talk station. Benny is kicking the back of my seat, and I reach back and grab his feet while waiting at a stop light. "Chill out, Benjamin," I say, regretting that sugary cereal.

"Yeah, Benny. Take a chill pill," Tiny says.

I snort. "Don't say that."

"Why not?"

"Because it's, like, talking about drugs," I tell her, taking a right turn, heading toward my mom's apartment. "It's not appropriate."

"Thomas says it."

"But we aren't in charge of Thomas, are we?"

A news story breaks through the pop culture chatter of the radio show hosts. "An accident on Highway 12 has created southbound traffic delays. A semi-truck hit the guardrail on exit 93, just after Steven's Pass. Update to follow."

I grit my teeth; I hate stories about accidents, especially those involving semi-trucks. After getting gas, I turn into the parking lot of my mom's complex, and I tell the kids to behave.

"I mean it, Grandma still has to work today. You need to be helpful, okay? If you're good, she'll take you swimming."

"We promise," Tiny and Benny say in unison as I park the van. Tiny may be more compliant than Benny, but I

3

know I won the mom lottery with the pair of them. The least expected outcome of getting pregnant by a man I hardly knew was that I would fall in love with motherhood and my baby daddy in one fell swoop. But I did. I'm the luckiest girl who never once pictured herself so damn settled at twenty-five.

But here I am, lugging a tote bag filled with changes of clothes and swimsuits, books and sunblock into my mom's apartment. Full-on mom mode. That's me. Penny Stone, waitress, wife, mother of two. Living a dream . . . just not the dream I ever imagined for myself. This is a far cry from a Paris bistro sipping rosé, with a pencil and notebook, scribbling my thoughts as I sit at a table for one. No customers for me to wait on in sight.

"Mom?" I call out, opening her unlocked door. The apartment is tidy, small and outfitted in cast-offs that tenants have left over the years.

The moment I enter her place, I walk to the sliding glass doors, pull them open. The air in here is always so heavy, even though I know she's making an effort not to smoke in front of the kids.

She's on the phone and holds up a manicured finger as we come inside; a weekly stop at the nail salon for a fill and polish is her only real indulgence. I think she was disappointed that I was never up for mani-and-pedi dates. Her only daughter — only child — and I never cared much for sparkly things. Clementine, though, fulfills Mom's need to pamper a girl in pink. I don't care, and Clementine loves it. Benny can be my sidekick, though to be fair, he's already walking to a shelf and pulling down a bin of dolls.

Stubbing out her cigarette into an ashtray, she ends the call. "Sorry, number eight needs maintenance. Dishwasher is busted."

"It's fine, I know you have to work today. Thanks for watching the kids. I didn't want to pass up the shift."

"It's fine." She waves a hand in the air. "Managing this place is easy, you know that."

4

And I do. I spent my last few years of high school living here, just Mom and me. "The kids are hoping to swim later. They promise to be good, don't you?" I give them raised eyebrows. They're already on the floor opening the plastic bins filled with Barbies, my childhood leftovers Mom was smart to preserve.

Mom smiles, kneeling on the worn carpet with Clementine and Benjamin. "How are my two favorite people doing today?"

Tiny smiles up at her. "Papa comes home tonight."

Mom looks over her shoulder at me, her lips frosted in CoverGirl pink, and she gives me the smile I've seen every single day of my life. Ledger is gone all the time as a long-haul truck driver, but Mom? She's my constant.

"Whatcha hanging around for, Penny?" she asks, shooing me off. "Don't you have work?"

I laugh. "Okay, fine, I'll go. Thanks again."

"Love you, Mama!" the kids say as I lean down to kiss their cheeks.

"Love you more," I say, pulling open the front door. I walk away, hearing their shouts as I go. *Impossible*, they holler, thinking they love me most. But they don't. They couldn't.

Ledger, my twins and my mom are my whole wide world, and I pray to God nothing ever changes that.

CHAPTER 2

Over Easy has an afternoon lull and I'm taking advantage of it in the mid-day sunshine. I'm sitting on the back steps with a Diet Coke, my notebook in my lap. I'm writing a list of short story ideas. The last four I submitted to magazines were rejected. And that means *every* story I've ever written has been rejected.

I'm starting to realize I don't know what I'm doing. The rejections from the editors tell me to look for a stronger hook, to find my authentic voice, to dig deeper and discover my true story. I read each rejection, blinking back tears, wanting validation that this effort is worth it somehow. Wanting someone to tell me that pursuing my champagne dreams on a beer budget isn't a waste.

Cheryl, my long-time manager, joins me outside, carrying a paper-lined basket of chicken strips and fries. I close my notebook and set down my pen, reaching for a fry.

"When does Ledger get back?" she asks, plucking a piece of chicken and dipping it in ketchup. Her shoulder-length hair is frizzy from bleach, and her eyes are rimmed in thick black liner. Her smile, though, is completely natural.

"I texted him a few minutes ago, asking when he'll be home. He hasn't replied." I groan, retying my unruly black hair into a bun on the top of my head. "I'm so ready to see him. It's been a long two weeks. Summer is stretching out forever." I look up to the blue sky, the sun hanging high. It's nearing ninety today and I wish I could strip out of my dress. This red-and-white polyester uniform is an inferno. When I get off work, maybe I'll put on a swimsuit and jump in the pool at Mom's. The twins would love that.

"I don't know how you do it, girl." Cheryl's twice my age. She gave me my one and only waitressing job when I was fifteen. Ten years later, I'm still her go-to girl. I don't think that's the story the editors of these literary magazines want.

I break a fry in half. "It's not so bad. I mean, it could be worse."

Cheryl clucks her tongue. "True. You and Ledger both got work, adorable kids, a marriage that makes every girl in town jealous."

"Shut up." I laugh, cocking my eyebrow at her. "I'm not sure anyone gives me a second look."

Cheryl stands, her face softening as she looks down at me. "Well, I see you, Penny. And I know you pretty well. Enough to know Ledger is lucky to have you, keeping that family of yours together while he's gone."

"Thanks," I say, brushing off her comment with a sheepish smile. After she goes back to the kitchen of the diner, I reread my story ideas as I finish my food. Adding a new one to my list: what it's like to be married to a long-haul trucker.

That might appeal to someone?

Twenty minutes later, after I've scrolled through Facebook and Instagram, called Mom to check in with her, there's still no reply from my husband.

When the phone finally buzzes, I answer without looking to see who it is. I haven't talked to Ledger since last night when he was going to bed. Allergies had been irritating him as he drove through eastern Washington — there's so much pollen in the air — and he'd grabbed Benadryl at a gas station before settling in to sleep in his cab at a truck stop.

"Are the twins in bed?" he'd asked, lying on his mattress as we FaceTimed. Pictures that Tiny and Benny colored for him in magic marker on white printer paper were taped to the wall, his head propped on the pillow I bought him for Christmas. It's printed with the words *I like your beard*. I sleep with one that says *I like your butt*.

"Yeah, for an hour." I walked around the kitchen, phone screen facing me as I finished tidying up the house for the day.

"What are you doing now?" he asked.

"I'm going to try and read a book I checked out at the library today. *Short Story Writing For Dummies*."

"Stop, Pen. Don't say that."

"Why?" I blew air out of my cheeks, frustrated. "I don't know what I'm doing, Ledger. I'm making it all up as I go."

"Maybe when the twins start school next year, you can start community college?"

"Maybe," I said. "But Bethany is taking classes right now and she's in over her head. Always stressed."

"Yeah, but she has a six-month-old and a toddler. You'll have all day."

I rolled my eyes, walking to our bedroom. "You mean when I'll be working at the diner?"

"I might have another raise by then, babe. You can cut your hours back."

I smiled tightly, pulling back the comforter on the bed. Biting my tongue. Not wanting to hurt him. But what I was thinking was that if I cut my hours, we'd always be paycheck to paycheck. Was it wrong to want more?

"I met someone at a diner this morning," he said.

I swallowed. Remembering the night I met him at a diner. "Yeah? Was she wearing a polyester uniform?"

He chuckled. "No, it was a college kid, just came back to the States after traveling abroad for a year. Called it a gap year. You ever heard that term?"

I looked away, not wanting him to see my eyes. The regret in them. Not for our marriage, our children . . . but for what wasn't. What could never be. I made a choice that changed my life. I fell in love with a man before I ever spread my wings.

Now, on nights like this, it felt like my wings were clipped. And the thing that's hard to accept is that I was the one who did the clipping. I had a savings account, a map, a plan. And instead of traveling Europe, I bought two cribs, a double stroller and a nursing bra.

It's not regret, it's just . . . a loss of what could have been.

We ended the call, Ledger and I, both of us saying I love you. And we do. We may not be loaded, but we have one another. It's not a gap year, it's a lifetime.

Now, on the steps outside the diner, I take the call from the unknown number, knowing I really ought to get back to work.

"Is this Penelope Stone?" a man I don't recognize asks, his tone causing me to sit up straighter. I set down my half-empty can of soda.

"Uh, yes, this is she."

"This is State Trooper Jordan Parrish, calling about an accident—"

I cut him off, panic setting in. "Accident?" The hot summer air is thick. It's hard to breathe as I absorb his words. "What kind of an accident?"

"Penny," Cheryl shouts from inside the restaurant. "Come in, you've gotta see this. The news. Oh, God, sweetheart."

"Yes, Mrs. Stone," Parrish says. "There was an accident involving your husband."

CHAPTER 3

Phone pressed to my ear, I walk into the crowded diner, my body moving toward the television, passing our loyal customers — men in ball caps with the insignias of their time in the service. Sheriff Lawson in the corner. I don't offer them my usual friendly smile. Cheryl holds a remote and turns up the volume; everyone in Over Easy is transfixed by the breaking news.

"Local law enforcement say this crash is more catastrophic than any they have seen in recent years," the reporter on the scene says, his expression grim, his tone tense. My heart falls. "A Grand Slam Transit semi-truck went over the guardrail near the Marshadow Pass, at mile marker 141. The carriage plummeted down the gorge."

I gasp, clutching my cell phone as I take in the images on the television. A helicopter is high above a massive, winding gorge that towers with layered rock walls in varying shades of gray and brown and black, the remains of the truck half-submerged in the rushing river below.

"Is he . . . Did he . . ." Tears fall from my eyes as Officer Parrish tells me what I'm seeing on screen is in fact Ledger's truck.

"His body hasn't been recovered. There is a team headed down to the site as we speak, and we will keep you updated with any information we have."

I sink to the floor; the diner has gone quiet, no clanging of forks or calling out of orders. Everyone in this place has known me for years. They are as glued to the television as I am.

A photo of my husband flashes on the screen. "Driver Ledger Stone has worked for Grand Slam Transit for the last three years. Reports show a clean record, and we are still waiting for a statement from his company. As we speak, search and rescue is descending the gorge to recover the body of Stone."

"Ma'am?" Parrish says loudly through the phone, and I wonder how many times he has asked for me before I heard him. "Do you hear me?"

"Yes, I'm here," I whisper, the room spinning as I search for words to say.

"Are you alone?"

I look around. "No, I'm at work."

"Good, stay with people who can support you; right now, that is the best thing you can do."

"Is he dead?" I ask.

"Mrs. Stone, as of now, no body has been found. However, the river has a fast-moving current this time of year and—"

"You think he's dead?"

The line goes quiet. "Ma'am—"

I cut him off, dropping the phone. The sob that leaves my mouth is deeper, more primal than any sound I have ever made in my life.

No.

No. Not Ledger. Not my rock. My anchor. My one true thing.

No.

Cheryl is on the floor with me, wrapping me in her arms. I let her hold me, scared of being swept away if she lets go. My body shakes as someone mutes the news. An unfamiliar hush fills the greasy diner. Burnt coffee sits in the air and tears fall on the weathered faces of men who spend their hard-earned military retirement on steak and eggs, tucking a generous tip in my apron on the first of the month.

I don't know how long I sit there on the linoleum floor. But when I finally stand, I reach for my purse. "Call my mom," I say to no one in particular. They all know who I'm talking about. Mom's as townie as I am. There's no way I can speak to her on the phone. "She needs to bring the kids home."

Cheryl won't let me drive. "You're shaking so bad you'll wreck the car." She catches herself, eyes filling with apology. There's no need to say sorry. Not over that. Not when Ledger is gone. Not when my life has just collapsed in one fell swoop.

I let her drive me. Because she's right. I could wreck the car with how badly I tremble.

And I can't do that. Tiny and Benny need me in one piece to get through this next part.

Whatever this next part may be.

* * *

The first part went like this: Five years ago, I was working a late-night shift at Over Easy. The place was empty, a half hour until closing. Johnny, the line cook, was in the kitchen cleaning the grill and I was wiping down tables, a freshly minted twenty-year-old in a too-short skirt because I wasn't above showing my thighs if it meant extra tips.

I was saving every spare dollar for my future. And the future was so shiny, it gleamed brighter than the tabletops as I washed them down with Clorox.

He came in when I was sweeping, my back to him, but when I turned, my heart snapped. Crackled. Popped. I was a Rice Krispies treat in human form the moment I looked into his forest-green eyes. Melting marshmallows and he knew it. And he didn't look away. That's the thing about Ledger Stone: he was never scared to look me in the eye. To say it

12

like it is. True blue, salt of the earth, honest-to-goodness, flannel shirt-wearing man. Mine.

I knew it before he did, I think. Knew that single night was going to change everything. Change me. He sat in the booth and I slipped in across from him and he didn't need a menu. It was obvious what he intended to order.

It all came to be without a single word: love at first sight. No one wants to hear all that. People ask how I knew, if what I'm saying is true. And I always answer the same. When I looked at him, I knew that he would never break me. And there were already so many parts that were broken. And all of them — the parts that had shattered when my father walked away after leaving Mom with one too many cracked ribs, when my first boyfriend hit me, when my second boyfriend hit harder — began to heal.

My mother said nothing heals that fast. And maybe that's true for most people. But I was never most people. And, it turns out, neither was Ledger.

"I'm Penny Carpenter," I told him, memorizing his face. His nose was crooked in a way that made his handsome features seem dangerous. A scar across the bridge of his nose, under his left eye. He'd seen trouble. Was trouble. Stubble on his strong jaw, arched dark brows. When he smiled at me, his teeth weren't perfectly straight and I liked that. His imperfection made him human, more accessible.

"I'm Ledger Stone." He offered me his hand and I shook it; our eyes locked and we both felt it. We talked about it later, how the world seemed to shift then, the axis changed. Our lives were moving in a new direction.

The road, though, was one we were both on. After my shift at the diner, I climbed into his Ford truck. He leaned over me and buckled me in, and I held my breath, knowing this was it. The stories I always wrote in my notebooks, about longing and desire, were suddenly more than a fantasy.

He turned on the radio and *Can't Help Falling In Love* came on, the velvety lyrics filling the cab. The song was so perfect for the moment I laughed. My whole life had felt like a struggle and then I met Ledger, and suddenly, it felt worth it. Like I could understand real love when I saw it because I'd been looking for it in the wrong places all my life.

"You don't like Elvis?" Ledger asked, eyebrow raised.

"Everyone likes Elvis." I looked at him, the neon lights from Over Easy illuminating us both.

"What else do you like, Penny Carpenter?"

I ran my fingers over the hem of my polyester uniform, the skirt above my knees. "I like long drives and slow dancing and summer nights."

He turned up the music and got out of the truck, and I closed my eyes, knowing what would happen next. Because I knew Ledger. Knew that he was the part of my heart I'd been missing. He opened my door and took my hand, and we danced under the stars.

"You're crazy," I told him, my heart catching in my throat. Scared. Everything I knew about men was bad. And you don't slow dance with a girl you just met, under a swollen moon, unless you're trouble.

"There are worse things to be," he said, spinning me around the parking lot.

"Like being alone," I told him, voice cracking, unable to hide my emotions. Not wanting to. He held my gaze and he understood. That giving my heart to someone was no simple thing. It was everything.

"You ever been in love?" he asked, his lips brushing against my ear.

"No."

"But you believe in it?"

I nodded, looking up at him, his hands slipping tighter around my waist, drawing me close. "I believe in all sorts of miracles."

He blinked back emotion then — but I saw the tears before he pushed them away. "So do I, Penny."

The song ended, and I stepped back. Knowing what was going to happen next didn't need to take place at the diner, I slid into the passenger seat, my heart racing.

"You always so skittish?" he asked, putting the truck in reverse.

I frowned. "I'm not skittish."

"You jumped like a rabbit."

"No. That was me being excited."

He laughed. "You always so honest?"

I nodded. "Always."

"Good."

"Are you?"

"I try to be." Ledger drove me to his motel, parked the truck. Killed the engine. "I don't do things halfway, Penny Carpenter. When I want something, I go all in."

"And you want me?"

He clenched his jaw, a smile impossible to suppress. "So damn bad." He took my hand in his and we walked to his room. Outside the door, he asked if I was sure.

"I've never been so sure in my life." It was the truth. I was so good at doubting who I was, what I was . . . Inside, I felt destined for big, beautiful things, but on the outside, I was a girl who didn't come from much and who just wanted a man to love her. Really, truly love her.

"What are you doing in Riverport?" I asked him, sitting on the edge of the motel bed.

"On my way home," he said. "Passing through town."

"And where is home?"

He sat down next to me on the bed, the weight of his body causing the cheap mattress to dip. Forcing me to fall closer to him. I was glad. I wanted to be closer. Close enough to kiss.

"Home isn't a place, it's a state of mind."

I smiled. "And your state of mind, Ledger, where is that?"

His lips met mine then, and we knew — we both did. All it took was one kiss and he'd come home. Ledger's place was with me.

* * *

15

"It's going to be okay," Cheryl says, driving toward my house, turning left down my street. "He's going to make it."

She grips the steering wheel so tight her knuckles have turned white. Her words don't comfort me at all because I saw the truck on the television screen. Destroyed and broken, just like all of our plans.

"You truly believe that?" I ask as my house comes into view — the house I share with the man I love, the man who is my home.

"I'm choosing to," Cheryl says. "Penny, you have to be strong. For the twins."

"I know I do," I say, my shoulders shaking. "But I'm not sure I know how."

Cheryl parks in my driveway, and it feels like the world has shifted again. Like the night Ledger and I met.

It feels like I'm falling again. But this time it's not love, it's loss.

And Ledger won't be there to catch me.

CHAPTER 4

Bethany watches from her front yard as Cheryl drops me off. She's barefoot with Neva tied to her chest in a sling. Even from my driveway, I see the concern in her eyes, the questions. "Will you go tell her?" I ask, pushing open the door of the Fiesta. "I can't deal with people, even my best friends."

"Of course," Cheryl says. Her eyes are rimmed with red, and she turns off the car. "You take care of yourself, Penny. Know we're all here for you."

Numb, I step over the green hose that winds around the half-dead grass of my lawn. The chipped paint on the front door is not exactly welcoming but certainly familiar. Inside my house, I groan, realizing I left the fans off this morning. The air is thick, the heat of the summer day persistent.

At the kitchen counter next to the fridge, I move aside the bowl of bruised apples I got at the Grocery Outlet and plug my phone into the charger, triple-checking that it's on full volume. I'm unable to process that Ledger won't be texting and apologizing for not calling sooner. That he won't tell me his phone died and he forgot to plug it in. That he loves me. That he loves Tiny and Benny. That he will be home soon.

So soon.

That he's only four hours away and that maybe we should get pizza from Romeo's tonight. He always orders extra cheese because that's what the twins love most.

It's impossible to believe he won't send another text two minutes later with emojis peppered with innuendo that make me blush and lick my lips, that make me think yes, thank God, he is coming home. Because being on the road for two weeks is two weeks too long. I miss him.

The front door opens and I startle, phone bouncing from my hands. My silent prayer that it will ring goes unanswered and I set it down, bracing myself for the onslaught of whatever comes next. Breaking my children's hearts; cracking them both open with a single sentence that can never, ever be taken back.

Mom rounds the corner, her face ashen, dropping her purse to the floor. She's the strongest woman I've ever known, but no one is strong enough for this. And she covers her mouth, gasping when she sees me. The kids are in their swimsuits, wet hair leaving droplets of water on the floor, as if my mother just pulled them from the pool. I wish that we could all go back to the complex, jump in the swimming pool and splash all day. I wish I could let them be children, but that is all about to change.

I can't protect them, and it's all I want. To keep them safe. Innocent. For just a minute longer. But more than that, I need them in my arms, breathing them in, refusing to let them go.

I fall to my knees and draw them close. My uniform clings to me the way I cling to them. My children need a father. Ledger has to be alive.

"I haven't told them yet," Mom says.

"What happened?" Benny asks in a whisper, his green eyes round and glassy.

Tiny's slender shoulders shake. I squeeze them harder. I know they are scared, but I'm scared too and I don't want to do this alone. I need Ledger.

"Papa was in an accident." My voice catches on the words as they leave my mouth. "A very bad accident."

"Is he gonna be okay?" Tiny asks, her voice so fragile, her words so tragic, that I want to scoop up each syllable and pretend they were never spoken. Put them away in the junk drawer with the duct tape and never look at them again. They are too awful to consider.

"They don't know," I manage to say. "The police and firemen are helping. They're looking for . . . for him."

Benny starts crying. Mom sits on the floor too. I hold them, all of them, and I can't let go. I don't know how long we sit like that, lost in the wave of emotion sweeping over my dirty kitchen floor. My house so hot, stale, my skin wet with sweat and salty tears.

Finally, Mom stands and turns on the TV.

"No," I croak.

"Please?" Benjamin says, transfixed by the story as the news comes on.

"We need to know, Penny. We need to know what's happening," Mom says.

Benny and Tiny are only four, but they understand the images. And maybe it's better this way. To see it for what it is. Honestly, it's better than me trying to explain. Better than their mother saying their father's truck went flying over a guardrail and that there is no body but really, how could anyone survive that fall?

It's not a story I want to tell. It's too ambitious. Too awful. Too real.

The stories I've written are silly, frothy, fun. Stories of money fixing problems and love wiping all the blues away.

Instead of talking, we watch the same story on repeat. Grand Slam Transit releases a statement, but the words are politically correct — a tragedy, investigating, our prayers are with . . . I can't listen.

When my phone rings, I grab it, answering without thinking because maybe it's Ledger. Maybe this was all a misunderstanding. It's not his truck. He's almost home.

"Hello?" I pant.

"Shit, Penny, I wasn't sure you'd answer." It's Jack Barrett, Ledger's closest friend. He got Ledger his job at Grand Slam three years ago, shortly after they met, and they've been thick as thieves ever since.

"My mom's here," I manage to say. "We've been watching the news."

Hearing his voice feels like a hard rock of reality hitting me in the stomach. I know wishing this away won't make it come true. And hearing Jack on the phone makes it feel all too real. We don't talk like this. We talk when Jack comes over to help Ledger in the garage, rebuilding an engine. We talk when Jack comes for dinner, throwing Benny in the air so high I look away, Ledger laughing, his hand on my waist. We don't talk like this: one on one.

"God, you should turn that off," he says. "Ledger would hate you seeing this."

I walk down the hall, pressing my forehead to the wall, my voice soft, cracking. "Do you think he survived?"

"I sure as hell hope so. You need anything? I can come over."

"I'm okay for now. Thanks, though," I say, shaking as I walk back into the kitchen, sinking back to the floor, my back against the refrigerator.

"If you do," he says, "I'm here for you."

"Thanks," I say, my voice paper-thin. "But be honest, do you think . . . do you think there might be a chance that he's . . ."

"Alive?"

"Yeah."

The line is quiet. Jack isn't a talker; that's why he and Ledger got along so well. The two of them could hang out all day, cracking open Bud Lights, listening to a ball game, never saying a word.

"I hope he is," Jack finally says.

"Me too." I look over at my children now asleep on the floor in front of the television. My mother is carrying dishes to the kitchen sink. She holds Benny's long-forgotten break-fast bowl. Her eyes meet mine as I finish the call.

"He can't be gone, Mom."

She sets the dishes in the sink and kneels, wrapping me into a hug. "The video footage looks pretty final, Penny."

I pull back, wiping my eyes. My hair falling wildly into my face, the house so hot, the day stretching out so long. It's only three in the afternoon. How will I get through this? One never-ending day after the next with Ledger never walking in through the front door.

"There's a chance," I say, my voice cracking.

Fuck realism. I'm choosing hope. Crazy, lovesick hope.

He can't be dead.

And if he's alive somehow, some way, he needs us to believe in him.

CHAPTER 5

I tell myself this isn't hard.

I can hold onto hope that my husband is still alive. Ledger is a truck driver. He leaves for long stretches of time. It's easy to pretend this is just like that. The trip is just slightly longer than we expected. My real regret is that I didn't think of this charade before the children saw the news. Because then they could play make-believe along with me.

I tuck them into Benjamin's bed, kissing their freckled cheeks, their upturned noses. I brush their curly black hair away and kiss their foreheads.

"I love you, and Papa loves you, and nothing will ever, ever change that," I tell them.

"Love you more," they say.

"Love you most." They have their own rooms, but tonight they want to be together. I don't argue. I let them snuggle and dream and stay close because, in the end, this is all we have. Each other.

I need Ledger at home.

"This isn't healthy," Mom says as I walk into the kitchen. I don't need her to elaborate.

I'm putting my energy toward convincing myself he's not dead. She's putting hers toward eradicating every germ from our house. Toilets, sinks, floors. The house smells comforting, like lemons and bleach. I let her hug me.

I nestle my chin on her shoulder and I blink, looking out the kitchen window. The grass needs to be cut. My ambitious summer plan of homegrown vegetables wilts in the wooden beds Ledger built me for Mother's Day. The front yard is mostly dead from the summer heat, but the back yard has lots of shade, and the grass is lush, thick, long. I have an urge to drag the lawnmower from the garage, rev the engine, and chop it all down. To drown out the noise in my heart with the hum of the motor.

"You're not saying anything." Mom's words bring me back to the moment. A sponge is in her hand and she sprays the counter with disinfectant, swiping away the germs.

"What would I say?" I ask, pulling open the fridge and grabbing the box of white wine. I pull out two coffee cups and fill them both. Mom shakes her head, refusing the mug that has the words *Write Epic Shit* on the front. Ledger gave it to me for Christmas. He was trying to be encouraging. At the time, it felt like pressure; now it feels like I want to wrap it in tissue paper and never let anyone use it again. What if there is never another Christmas gift from him?

I pour the contents of her mug into mine and take a sip of the cardboard-tasting pinot grigio.

"I don't know," she says, sighing, sitting down at the table, her fingernails tapping the wooden tabletop. "You could call your friends? Let people know?"

I shake my head. "Your phone has been buzzing all night. I'm sure you've let anyone who needs to know, know."

"It's on Facebook, the local Riverport page is blowing up about it. So many people care about you, about the kids. Everyone is heartbroken for you, Penny."

I take a long sip of wine, settling into a kitchen chair opposite her. "We don't know he's dead."

"Sweetheart." Mom reaches across the table for my hand. I pull back. I can't go there. Not yet. It's like ever since I got the call, I've been transported back in time to when

Ledger and I met. The miracle of it, of him coming into the diner that night when he could have stopped at Denny's or a burger joint and instead, he came to Over Easy. He slid into a booth across from me and ran his hand over his scruffy jaw and smiled. A smile I will never, ever forget.

"I know it sounds crazy," I tell her, believing the words I say. "But I'd know if he was dead, Mom. I'd feel it."

Mom nods, wiping her eyes. "I don't want you to hold onto false hope."

"They're still looking for his body."

"The truck went into a river, Penny."

"So?"

"So," she says slowly. "Measure your expectations."

I hear her, I do. But I don't want to listen. The silence is thick and the August air is so hot and heavy and I just want to sleep with a dozen fans pointed at my face. When I wake, maybe this will all have passed. The heat and the accident. It will all have been a bad dream. A nightmare. This isn't my life. It can't be. Not when Ledger and I haven't done any of the things we planned. He can't be gone when we've only just started.

"Want me to stay the night?" Mom asks. "I could sleep on the sofa. I'm not sure you should be by yourself."

I don't want her here, though; I want to sleep believing Ledger will be here when I wake. In my bed. I want to sleep with the hope of Ledger coming into the house late at night, sliding under the sheets. His breath warm as he kisses my neck, his hands running over my body as he tells me all about how much he missed me.

I tell Mom no. "I'm usually home alone when Ledger's on the road."

"I understand, but this isn't usually, Penny," she says, her voice fraught with worry. "This is all new territory."

I stand, having finished my wine, grateful for all she's done today. "Thanks, Mom, but I just want to be by myself." I close my eyes, not wanting to cry. If I start crying again, it will feel like I've given up. "Sorry."

"Don't apologize," she says. "I need a smoke anyway and Lord knows you won't let me here."

"I love you," I tell her as we walk to the front door. "I'll call tomorrow. Maybe the police will have news by morning."

She gives me one last hug before walking away. When she's gone, I check on the twins. They're both out cold. Then I go to the garage and I pull out the lawnmower and I squeeze the handlebar as the motor hums to life, vibrating. My body shakes. I said I wouldn't cry, but I chop the long grass in the backyard until the tears fall so hard I can't see.

* * *

When I wake, I roll over, my hands stretched out across Ledger's side of the bed. I sink my face into his pillow. It smells like him. His sweat, his skin. This is where I want to stay, in this smell, in this promise. The kids are awake, tiptoeing into my room, Benny's round eyes peeking around the door, Tiny clasping a stuffed bunny to her chest. I pat the bed, needing them to crawl in with me. Stay with me. Mom was right. I shouldn't be alone.

"I need Papa to be home soon," Benny says. "He was going to teach me how to ride my bike."

My arms wrap around them, and I kiss the tops of their heads, threading my fingers through their thick curls. If he's really gone, I have no idea how in the world I am going to survive this. Life without him. It won't be fair. I've had hundreds of mornings like this. In our bed, with our kids. Slow, easy mornings with rumpled hair and rumpled sheets, and he hasn't. He has been on the road, working, missing everything. Missing so damn much, it makes my chest ache, and I start to cry.

I cry more of those tears I was determined not to shed, and they won't stop.

Clementine wipes my cheeks and tells me, "Don't cry, Mama. It's okay, Mama."

I want to believe her, to think this *is* okay, but it's not. If Ledger is gone, then nothing will ever be okay again.

There's a knock on the door. The doorbell rings. I reach for my phone. I missed texts from my coworkers, Jack, my cousin Ellen — all of them checking in, sending their love. One from Bethany, too. *Dropping off breakfast. Leaving it on the porch. Love you.*

My stomach rolls, and I realize I didn't eat dinner. "Bethany brought us breakfast," I tell the twins. "Let's go get it." I reach for my pale pink terrycloth bathrobe and slip my feet into plastic flip-flops. Better than slippers; I can run out to the store in them.

Padding down the hall, I rub my eyes, mascara caked on the corners, and I pull my curls into a hair-tie before opening the door. It already feels hot, and I call to the twins to turn on the fans.

Homemade muffins and sliced fruit and chocolate milk fill a tote bag, but that isn't what I see first.

A woman I've never seen before stands on my front steps. Platinum and petite and wearing a perfect face of make-up. Are you fucking kidding me?

"It's not even eight in the morning," I tell her, grabbing the bag of food. "If reporters seriously think they can come here and—"

She cuts me off. "I'm not a reporter," she says.

"Then who are you? Because seriously, after the night I've had . . ."

"I'm Emma James," she says, pulling her shoulders back, eyes locked on mine. I try to look away, but her gaze is adamant. "You're Penny Stone, right? And you're married to Ledger? Ledger Stone?"

I nod.

"Well, here's the thing, Penny," she says, twisting her pink lips. "So am I."

CHAPTER 6

The words take a second to register.

Emma repeats herself. "I'm married to your husband, only . . . only he . . ." Tears fill her eyes as she tries to compose herself, to finish her words. She blinks, and I step away.

My chest tightens as I look at this woman who is the exact opposite of me in terms of appearance. She's cute and curvy with pink manicured nails and lash extensions. Every time she blinks, they flutter dramatically.

What the actual hell is happening? My hands tremble as my eyes search hers. Behind me, Clementine and Benny are asking what's for breakfast.

"I have to feed my kids."

She nods, wiping her eyes. "Right, of course. It's just, I saw the story on the news, his photo. I couldn't believe my eyes. I started driving at five this morning, the moment I woke up."

I look over my shoulder at Benny and Tiny. "Can you give me a second?" I ask, not wanting a stranger in my house — a stranger who says she's married to my husband.

Inside, I grab the food from Bethany and pour the kids glasses of chocolate milk. I set muffins and fruit on plates and flip on the television, pulling up Netflix and starting a show for them. "I'll be on the front steps talking to that lady, Emma. All right?"

"Who is she?" Tiny asks, peeling back the paper lining of the muffin.

I swallow. Ledger has never been married before me. It's only ever been me. Ledger and me against the world, hands held, against all odds. There was never another woman.

She must be crazy.

"She's, uh, she's a friend of Papa's," I say, choosing my words slowly.

They nod solemnly as I blink back tears, then they sit on the floor with their plastic plates and plastic cups and stare at the screen.

Outside, Emma is standing just where I left her, wringing her hands together. "Sorry," I say, trying to collect myself. "I just don't understand."

She pulls out an envelope from her designer purse. A stack of photos in her hands. We sit down on the steps, and she hands them to me, one at a time.

It's Ledger, that's for sure. Same green eyes, dirty brown hair. Same dimples in both cheeks, the same ones Benny and Tiny have. Same scar across the bridge of his nose. Same teeth. Same smile. Same everything.

"Where did you get these?"

She hands me more, silently. Photos of her in an ivory gown. A small church. A wedding. Their wedding. Emma looking up into Ledger's eyes, a man a foot taller than her, making vows. Cutting the cake and dancing. It's the wedding I never had.

We went to the courthouse. My mom was the witness, and I didn't even wear white. I wore wedge sandals and a denim dress and my hair was wild and loose, the way Ledger likes it. Has always liked it. We stood nearly eye to eye, and when he slipped a ring on my finger, we both cried. Promises were made.

Was it all a lie?

"I don't understand," I say. "He never told me he had been married. Why would he lie about that . . . about you?"

28

I stare at the picture of the two of them, looking as in love as we had been on our wedding day.

Emma tucks a strand of her long, straight hair behind her ear. "This is going to be a shock to you. When I saw the news, it shocked me too. Scared me, really. It was like seeing a ghost."

"What do you mean? A ghost?"

"His name isn't Ledger Stone," Emma says. "It's Henry James. And almost five years ago, he was in a car crash — his pickup went over a cliff. And his body was never recovered. He died in that accident. Went up in flames. Or at least, we thought he did. We all thought so. We had a funeral for him." She pulls out a folder, handing me the death certificate for Henry James and a marriage license. A paperclipped obituary. *Leaving behind his wife, Emma James.* "He was dead. But I think . . ." She starts sobbing into her hands. "I think he left me, Penny. My husband didn't die. He pretended to, and then he ran."

Blood drains from my face. And I feel ill. Dropping the photos, I lean over, retching into the grass. No. No. This can't be real.

Emma keeps crying. "I knew it was my Henry when I saw his face. And the crazy thing is I felt relieved. I never believed he died. It was love at first sight when we met, and if your soulmate was dead, you'd feel it, wouldn't you?"

Her words send a chill over me. My spine and my bones and my heart. Ice. "You think . . . you think this wasn't an accident? You think Ledger left me? That's why you came here?" I ask, my voice sharp as her story hits me. "You came here to tell me my husband is—" I stop talking, covering my mouth. The horror of her story is setting in. I can't believe this — this can't be happening. Ledger loves me. He would never, ever leave me.

But as I look at Emma, small and shaking, I realize she feels the exact same way.

Soulmates. Love at first sight. Was it all canned lines? What was real?

29

"When did he die?" I ask. "I mean, when did he have his accident?"

"April 14, 2015," she says. "The worst day of my life."

"We were already . . . Ledger and I had already met . . . We . . ." Shame floods me. I slept with a man who was married. Then I married him myself.

"I knew it," she says, crying harder now. "When did you meet him?"

"He came into the diner in February of that year. He was traveling through for work, staying at a hotel after giving a training at an auto dealership a few towns over. He was a service technician instructor for General Motors. At least that's what he said. He lost his job a few months after we met."

"Lost it?" Emma scoffs, pained. "He didn't have the job anymore because everyone thought he had died." She runs her fingertips under her eyes. "He was gone so much for work, but I never thought he was a cheater. I thought he loved me."

I nod, piecing the horrible story together. "We didn't see each other much. That first night, we . . . well, I fell in love with him. He only came through town twice more before I told him I was pregnant. That was April 12. I'd never forget it because it's my birthday. He came to the diner and we ate cake, and then I told him."

"So you have a child with him?" Emma asks, pulling back, looking at me more critically.

"Yeah. Uh, twins. They're four."

Her lips form a firm line.

A fresh wave of nausea washes over me as I consider Ledger having a child with another woman. With this woman. A woman so different from me, it makes my head hurt.

She looks at me blankly, as if I have something to ask her. But the truth is I'm not ready to know if there are other kids in the picture. Motherhood has always been such a complicated thing for me.

I never meant to get pregnant. Falling in love with Ledger was one thing, but having his children was quite another. We always thought we'd have time later to travel the world, to fill a backpack with a Europass and go.

But now everything has changed. Ledger is missing, and Emma's husband is dead. And she was his wife. And so, then, what am I?

"So you told him you were pregnant and then he drove back home," Emma says calmly as if the story is becoming more concrete in her mind. "And then one day later, he left me for you. He faked his death and took on a new life and . . . never looked back."

I draw in a breath, not knowing what to make of her words. How could everything I thought I knew about my life be a lie? My Ledger wouldn't do this to me. Would he?

"So if he's gone, faked his death again, then my question is," Emma says, sitting up straighter, biting her bottom lip, "where is wife number three?"

CHAPTER 7

"I need coffee for this," I say, entering the house. The kids don't turn from their show, and I tell Emma to help herself to breakfast as I start a pot.

She picks up a muffin, her heels click-clacking as she inspects the family photos hanging on the wall. I watch her take in my life, this life with her husband. She looks so polished, poised. In a white button-up blouse and dark denim jeans. Toned arms. Tan. Her Burberry purse a status symbol I can't exactly identify with.

I'm momentarily grateful my mom cleaned the house top to bottom last night in her manic response to Ledger's accident. But then, pouring coffee, I berate myself. Why the hell do I care if my kitchen is clean for this woman? My husband is dead.

She is also linked to me in ways that are just dawning on me, and the facts are too solid to lead me to believe she is fabricating any of this. We both married the same man. The death certificate listed his date of birth — June 8. Same as I always knew it to be.

Is my marriage even valid? I grab creamer from the fridge, hands shaking as I absorb that shock. It was all a sham.

"Did you really not know?" she asks. "About me, his real name, any of it?"

I shake my head, offering her a mug of coffee before lifting mine to my lips, wondering what she must think of me. "I didn't know a thing."

"He's a lying bastard," she says. "That piece of shit," she mutters before apologizing when she remembers the kids. "Do you mind if I use the restroom? It was a long drive and I'm a hot mess right now."

I show her to a bathroom before going to my bedroom and pulling on a bra, then slipping a black cotton jersey dress over my head. The color and fabric are forgiving, and as I brush my teeth in the attached bathroom, I think just how unforgiving I feel. What the fuck is Ledger up to? This isn't him. The man I know. But Emma's words are simple, direct, and the proof is in the photos. The scar cutting across the bridge of his nose.

"How did you get that?" I asked him the first night we met, in the motel bed, my finger tracing the scar. I was already so wrapped up in him, his arms holding me tight.

"An accident when I was ten. My foster brother and I were sword fighting with sticks." Ledger laughed. "He won."

Now I splash cold water on my face, looking hollow and red-rimmed, memories surfacing too fast. I feel like I'm drowning, like a woman whose husband just died. Whose husband just left. Whose husband she never really knew.

My phone buzzes. I grab it, thankful it's my mother. I close the door halfway as I tell her, with shaking breaths, what I've just learned.

"What in God's name," Mom mutters. And I squeeze my eyes shut. Not wanting to face this. Any of it. I want my husband here to explain this all away.

"I know." I exhale, trying to remain calm. The last thing the kids need is me in meltdown mode. "According to Emma, he faked his death after I told him about the pregnancy, Mom. He left his wife for me. But it's worse than that. She thinks he's doing the same thing right now. That it's me he's left this time." I run a hand through my hair. "It's weird, right, both car crashes?"

"You trust her?" Mom asks. I hear the pull on her cigarette. Can practically smell the smoke through the phone. "What if she's batshit, Pen? Be smart about this. Where is she right now?"

I draw in a sharp breath and push open my bedroom door. I run down the hall to find Emma on the floor with the kids, as Tiny and Benny show her their Legos and Barbies that are spread out on the living room carpet.

Emma's eyes meet mine, a soft smile on her face. "They wanted to show me their toys."

I nod, pointing to the phone. "Just taking a call. Give me a sec?"

She gives me an understanding nod and turns back to Benny, who is demonstrating his rocket launcher.

I step out of the front door, keeping it open. "I don't even know what I do from here."

There's another call coming in. Grand Slam Transit flashes on the screen. "I gotta go. It's his work. Maybe they have an update."

"How about I come over and get the kids, bring them here to go swimming?"

"Don't you have work?" I ask.

"Penny, I took the week off, obviously. Your husband is . . . Well, he's not here."

The other line keeps ringing. "Right. Okay, see you soon."

I hang up with her and accept the other call, but it's too late. They're already leaving a voicemail.

"Hello, Penny. This is Vance Donovan, an internal investigator for Grand Slam Transit. I know you've had a rocky twenty-four hours, but if you can give me a call as soon as possible, that would help everyone move forward with this case."

I frown, staring at the phone. The word *case* feels so heavy, so final. I expect the police to call it a case, but Grand

34

Slam? From them I expect condolences. Walking back into the house, I ask Clementine and Benjamin if they had enough to eat.

"Yeah," Benny says, carrying his empty dishes to the sink. "Bethany's muffins are good."

I tousle his hair, wrapping my arms around him, thinking that I should probably go talk to my neighbor. She's probably freaking out. And she doesn't even know the half of it. She wanted a wine night to dish on Joanne and Marty's split — but the gossip about my life is one hundred percent more provocative. My marriage may be written entirely in lies.

"Grandma's on her way over," I tell him. "She's gonna take you swimming again at the apartment."

Clementine perks up at this. "Really?"

I nod. "Yep, so go put on your suits, and brush your teeth and hair, okay?"

Tiny bites her lip. "Mama, are you gonna be okay without us?"

I kneel on the floor, pulling the pair into my arms. "I have some people to talk to today, people trying to find Papa, okay?"

"Okay," Tiny says, her voice so small. "But first, can we call him?"

Benjamin nods. "Yeah, we can tell him we love him in case he's lost and trying to get home."

My heart aches at their innocence, their hope. The same sort of hope I held last night, in the early morning hours. The hope I had before Emma arrived on my doorstep and turned my world upside down. Everything can change so damn fast, in the blink of an eye.

"Sure," I say, grabbing my phone. "Let's call him and let him know we love him."

He may not be the man I thought I knew, but he's still their father — there's no doubt about that. And our children deserve to love him without the bitter facts I'm trying to swallow.

35

I place the call on speakerphone, and as it begins to ring, I'm very aware of Emma, stepping closer to us in the kitchen. Tears fill her eyes again as she stands perfectly still, listening as the call goes to voicemail.

"Hey, it's Ledger here. Sorry I missed your call. I'm probably busy watching *The Bachelor* with Penny or rolling around on the floor with the twins. Catch ya soon!"

"Hi, Papa," Tiny says, her bottom lip trembling. "I love you. And I miss you."

Benny scrunches up his little face, trying hard to be brave. "I love you, Papa. I hope you're coming home soon."

Tears flood my eyes. I look up, meeting Emma's gaze. Her expression is unbearable, and I can only imagine what it would be like to hear the voice of the man you believed was dead.

The twins end the call, and I retrieve my phone. "I'm sure when Papa hears that, he will be so happy," I tell them, unsure of what else to say. The fact remains that I'm holding my shit together right now for one reason and one reason alone: them.

They head to their rooms to get dressed and I rub my eyes. Exhausted and it's not even nine a.m.

"I should go," Emma says, reaching for her purse. "I barged in on you, and I know this is a lot to process."

"No," I say. "Don't go. If what you say is true, it's up to us to find Ledger."

CHAPTER 8

Mom comes and gets the twins, her face blotchy, concern written in her eyes. I doubt she's slept at all.

"I'll be okay, I just have to figure this all out," I tell her. We're standing at her car, and I hand her a bag with towels and life jackets. "I don't know what to think."

Mom clucks her tongue as I buckle in the twins. I exhale as she pulls open the driver-side door. "You need to call the cops about this, if he faked his death before, Penny, that's important for them to know."

"Is it?" I question. "If I tell them this, I can't backtrack later. I need to make sure I don't say something, *do something* I shouldn't. Ledger isn't a stupid man. I trust him. He would have his reasons."

"You trust him after what she said?"

"I don't know Emma from anyone," I say, rubbing my temples. "And you said it yourself yesterday, the crash was a terrible accident. You were sure he was dead, telling me I needed to face the facts."

"Right, but Penny, now the facts have changed."

I try to focus on what I know. "I love him, Mom. He can't be gone. He would never do this to me."

Mom's eyes narrow. She slams her door shut so the kids can't hear and leans over the roof of her car. "Penny, I know you loved Ledger, but we all know that he wasn't exactly stable."

My throat goes dry. "Don't, Mom. I can't."

"Penny," she says more gently. "He's always had issues. Maybe—"

"Mom," I say, my voice tight, clipped. "Not now. Please, I don't want to rehash a breakdown that happened three years ago. Please. Let it rest."

She nods, knowing I'm not emotionally capable of going there. Ledger may not have been perfect, but he was perfect for me. I'm not ready to face the possibility that any part of our love story could have been fake.

He loved me. Loves me.

In the house, I find Emma standing in the kitchen with her arms crossed, her face blank, looking as numb as I feel.

"Hey," I say. "The kids are gone for the day."

"They're so sweet," she says. "Clementine is just a doll."

"She is. It's funny how, in life, sometimes the thing you never asked for is exactly what you need."

Emma gives me a sad smile. "Henry and I . . ." She stops, running her finger under her eye. "I'm sorry."

"Don't apologize." I want her to finish whatever she was saying — anything I can learn to understand the situation better will help.

"It's just, seeing the twins reminds me of . . . of the daughter Henry and I . . ."

My blood goes cold. There are so many things wrong with this situation, but the idea of Ledger having a child with another woman is one thing too many.

"We had a little girl, Eva. She died when she was an infant."

"Oh, God," I say, covering my mouth, feeling sick. This is going to put me past the breaking point.

"I know," she says, pressing her knuckles to her lips. "It's too complicated. I get that, Penny, I do. The person I loved . . . the man we both loved . . . it seems like it was all a lie."

"Ledger wouldn't—" I stop talking because what *can* I say? He wouldn't betray me? There must be something more to this story? Those words would devastate Emma — she's already reeling from so much loss. Not only did she bury her husband, but she buried her daughter.

"I'm so sorry to have barged in on your life like this," Emma says, taking a deep breath and attempting to regain her composure. "I know you want me to stay and start piecing this together, but I think I should go get a hotel, shower, regroup. I could grab us lunch and then come back once we've both had some time to process?"

It's not just my life that has been upended. She believed her husband was dead. That his body was burned in a car fire, lost forever. She grieved the death of a man I fell in love with, my soulmate.

"I just don't want you to leave my life as quickly as you entered it," I say. "It might sound crazy, but I feel like we need to talk. About all of this. Before I go to the cops."

She bites her bottom lip. "I want to talk with you too, but maybe the cops should be involved. I mean, what Henry did is a crime. Right?"

"I don't know what to think." I press my fingertips to my forehead. "You're right, though. I do need a second to process."

I pull her into a hug before she goes. She's my ally in some strange, twisted way. And she should hate me; I slept with her husband while they were still married. He got me pregnant with his twins. I realize, with a shaken sense of truth, that in this story she's telling, Ledger is the villain. He is the one who lied, cheated, broke her heart and is now breaking mine. The man I loved — *love* — might also be a man I don't know.

Alone, I look around my house, and my head spins. Each photograph hanging on the wall threatens what I know to be true — candid pictures of a happy family — but was he happy? The bed we slept in together with the twins nestled between us, now empty. The couch we binge-watched television on now looks cold. Everything surrounding me was written with the pretense of commitment. How can it be a life shaped by love when it began with such horrific lies?

There's a knock on the door and I pull myself together, not sure who it would be. Last time I answered the knock, it was Emma. The woman who just rewrote my entire narrative.

But standing on the doorstep is a familiar face. Jack Barrett walks in, coffee cups in a cardboard holder, and he wraps me in a hug. "Shit, Penny."

It feels good to have Jack here — I need to talk to him, really talk to him, before Emma comes back. If anyone knew Ledger, it's him.

"How are you holding up? Everyone at work is a wreck over this, and I couldn't go in, couldn't face seeing anyone. So I came here instead. Maybe it was a bad idea. I know he's your husband, but damn, you guys are the closest thing I've got to family."

"No, it's fine," I say, wiping my eyes and taking the iced caramel latte. "I could use the company."

"Yeah?" He pulls me into a hug and I hold onto him, closing my eyes, wishing it was Ledger. Wishing my husband was the one here to comfort me. When I step back, Jack clears his throat, runs a hand over his neck. "Maybe no news is good news?"

I take a sip of the latte, the rich caramel syrup coating my throat, and I blink back tears. "Maybe."

"See, Pen," he says, squeezing my hand. "It's gonna be okay."

Okay? Not with Emma in the picture, with my entire perspective suddenly off-kilter.

"Hey, don't cry," he says. "Ledger would be pissed if he knew I upset you."

I wipe my eyes, exhaling. "He hates seeing me cry. Remember when I sprained my ankle last Thanksgiving during our flag football game?"

"He carried you home like you were a baby." Jack smiles at the memory, and I feel my shoulders fall. "I've never seen him so worried."

"It was the same when the twins were born. He was a wreck at the hospital." I smile at the memory of my burly husband falling apart. "I yelled at him, *Ledger, it's childbirth, I'm supposed to be screaming.*"

Jack chuckles. "He loves you. He wants you to be happy."

My face falls suddenly, and I no longer have it in me to joke around. "Jack. We've got to talk. It's gotten really bad."

His face goes white and he pulls in a breath as if he's been preparing for this. "Did they find his body?"

I press my fingers to my lips, shaking my head tightly, wondering if Emma was right. Is Ledger with wife number three right now? As I sit here worried sick about him? "No," I tell Jack. "It's worse than that."

"How can it be worse, Pen? He's gone."

I lead him through the house, pulling open the sliding glass doors and walking out onto the patio. We did it all up last year with our tax return. Ledger got a grill, I got a table and chairs, an umbrella, the kids got a swing set. We felt like an all-American family. Like we were finally getting our shit together. We could have barbecues and invite the neighbors, and all the adults would have places to sit. We wouldn't have to sit with our potato salad and hamburgers in our laps.

Bethany and Leo came over with their kids for the Fourth of July and we drank sangria, laughing over nothing, punch-drunk and happy. The kids drew with sidewalk chalk and ran around with sparklers. It was perfect.

Sitting here with Jack now, a little over a year later, the memory seems so make-believe. Was life ever so perfect as how I remember it? Even now, thinking harder, I can see the cracks in the story I told myself. Benny threw rocks at Tiny, fighting over a tricycle. I was irritated with Ledger over forgetting the hot dog buns, and Leo and Bethany were trying to figure out if they were going to stay together. She had no idea she was two months pregnant. Jack stopped by and got drunk, talking about how online dating was bullshit and how he wished he could find a girl like me.

I know he is fond of me, which is why I know he will tell me the truth, even if it's hard to swallow.

"I need to ask you something, Jack. And I need you to be honest with me. Don't edit yourself to protect Ledger. I need the truth."

Jack sets down his Frappuccino, leaning forward on his knees. "What is it, Penny? You're freaking me out."

"Did Ledger ever mention another woman? Another woman he might have been seeing?"

Jack stiffens. He closes his eyes, shaking his head. "Fuck," he says. "I knew it."

CHAPTER 9

My body goes rigid. "Knew what?" I ask. My voice sharp. Tight. Like I'm about to snap.

"It's gonna sound weird, but . . . about two weeks ago, I was with Ledger. We were at Joe's Pub — he was leaving in the morning for this last trip that he was just on. And anyways, he got this call. It was strange because he answered it right away, and you know how Ledger is about talking on the phone."

I nod, needing him to tell me the story faster.

"Well, anyways, the number flashed on his screen. Unknown. He stepped away to take the call, and when he came back to the table, I asked what was up. He said you called, needing him to get milk on the way home. I knew he was lying. Your photo and name come up on his phone when you call."

I lick my lips, trying to remember asking Ledger for milk. I can't. "Anything else?"

"Yeah, now this is gonna sound weird, okay? But the next day I saw you at Shop 'n' Save, remember? It was early in the morning, you had the twins, Ledger had already left. You were getting a box of donuts at the bakery. And you had a gallon of milk in your cart."

My blood goes cold. "I remember. You said, Ledger is really dropping the ball, something like that, right? You said, didn't you call asking for milk last night?" Jack nods, and I go on. "I remember shaking my head, confused at what you were saying. And you realized that whatever you were talking about, I didn't understand. You backpedaled."

Jack runs a hand through his short brown hair. "Ledger isn't like this. Lying over shit like milk. Making up stories. It's Ledger. He's as solid as any damn rock. I thought at the time, what the hell would he be lying to me for? I tried to think what he would keep from me, his closest friend. And all I could come up with was another woman. Because he knows how much I care about you, how I'd never let him live that down. Cheating on you would be a deal-breaker."

I draw back, arms crossed, not liking this version of Ledger. "You really think he was having an affair? All you have to go off of is one unknown number. One lie about milk."

Jack leans back, solemn. "You asked the question, Penny. Not me. What do you think?"

"I think Ledger has some explaining to do."

* * *

I fill Jack in on everything I know. Emma and the accident and his faked death, and by the end, he's pacing the patio, strung out on the facts. I show him the photographs Emma left. He looks them over, haunted by the story that I share.

"How much of it is real?" he asks. "I mean, do you actually believe the guy we love could have been totally fictional?"

I groan, my gut all twisted, my heart torn up. "I'm too scared to google the accident from five years ago."

"We have to," Jack says pulling out his phone. "What was his name?"

"Henry James, married to Emma. He died April 14 in Vancouver, Washington. He was a service trainer for General Motors." My tone is flat, unrecognizable. I tell Jack what I know as plainly as possible because if I give into my feelings right now, I might never recover. And my kids need me to be strong, to figure out what the fuck is happening with our lives.

"It's true," he says. "Everything she said. Look." He hands me his phone, and I read the *Vancouver Tribune*.

> *Local man dies in fatal crash over a cliff, body never recovered after being engulfed by flames. Henry James leaves behind wife, Emma.*

The photo attached of *Ledger* — Henry — is unmistakable. Same scar under his left eye that crosses the bridge of his crooked nose. It's my Ledger.

"Fuck, Penny, this is insane."

"Do you think he did it again? Left me for whoever was on the other end of that unknown number?"

"I don't know. I mean, shit, why would he do this, leave you? Penny, you're everything a guy could want. Thoughtful, smart and a damn good writer."

I swallow, handing Jack his phone and leaning away. I know Jack has always cared about me. Like if Ledger wasn't my husband, he might want to be. Not in a creepy way but in a kind way. Protective. In a way that makes me believe he's looking out for my best interests. And right now I need that. I need backup.

"I have to call Grand Slam. The claims guy left a message. I just don't even want to deal with that right now."

"Penny," Jack says slowly. "Listen, let me help. I can call them for you."

"I can't imagine Ledger doing this. Leaving me. I know our life wasn't perfect and that the kids were a lot and money was tight, but we were happy. At least, I thought we were happy."

Jack doesn't say anything. He looks away, as if my words are too pathetic considering everything we've just discussed. And maybe they are.

"You know how he was always talking about the brakes, how the trucks weren't being inspected properly?" I say, desperate now for Jack to look into my eyes once more. To track with me. My life is a whole new level of fucked up when I consider finding my husband's dead body the best scenario.

"Maybe it was an accident," I say. "Maybe he did die in that gorge. Maybe his body is in the river."

Jack reaches for my hand, squeezing it. "Maybe," he says, nodding at last. "Maybe Grand Slam is to blame for all of this."

The words seem empty, though, just like all of the promises Ledger made me.

CHAPTER 10

By the time Emma returns with lunch, I've showered and changed, and Jack is filling me in on the call he placed with Vance Donovan from Grand Slam.

"They're investigating the scene right now, trying to figure out if this was an accident or not." Jack walks into the garage to get some beers from the extra fridge out there.

"It wasn't," Emma says bitterly, setting down a bag of sandwiches and salads. She pulls out an envelope from her purse. "Hey, this is for you, Penny," she says softly, her tone having turned. "Some more photos of Henry, from when he was a kid."

My hand trembles as I take what she hands me. "Wow, I've never seen pictures of him when he was little."

Emma places a hand on my arm. "I thought that might be the case. Anyways, you don't need to look at them with me around, I just thought . . ."

I blink back tears. "No, that was very thoughtful. I've never seen Ledger as a child."

"What's wrong?" Jack asks, coming into the kitchen with Bud Lights. "What did you say to her?" he says to Emma, raising his voice.

"She didn't do anything," I say, tears falling down my cheeks now.

"What happened, Pen?" He rests a hand on my back. I turn to him, crying against his chest.

"He can't be gone, Jack. He can't be." My shoulders shake, and he wraps his arms around me, holding me tight.

"I know," Jack says. "He isn't."

I step away, wiping my face. "Sorry," I gasp. "It's just all so much to consider."

Emma clears her throat. "I was hoping to make you feel better, not worse."

Jack takes her in. "We're gonna figure out what really happened. Where he is. We're going to get a firm answer on that one way or another." I'm sure he's looking over her glossy hair and white teeth and polished nails. Or maybe not. Maybe I'm just fixated on those things because they are the details that contrast my shoestring budget life so sharply.

"It pisses me off, though," he continues. "They're more concerned with whether or not this is their fault because they know if it's on them, there's gonna be hell to pay in terms of a lawsuit. They'll owe you more than a pretty penny if they've fucked up here."

My stomach rolls. I rush to the bathroom, hating the idea of getting a settlement over Ledger's death. I drop the envelope of photos on the tiled floor and lean over the toilet, sickened with my twisted hope that this was in fact an accident.

That it was Grand Slam's fault. Because that would mean my husband didn't run away from our life.

And somehow, as I sit on the cold tiled floor of my bathroom, an accidental death at the hands of his employer seems better than him being alive and simply leaving his family.

I lock the bathroom door, leaning against it, keeping the light off. Closing my eyes. Trying to hide. My thoughts, though, won't let me be.

"Penny." Jack's at the door. "Your neighbor, Bethany, is here."

"Tell her I'm asleep. That I can't do this. Can't do anything."

"Hey," she says through the door, and I know she heard me. "I just want you to know I love you. I'm here, okay?"

"Okay," I tell her, massaging my temples. Grateful I don't have to explain. As far as she knows, my husband is dead and I don't have to explain that. "Love you too."

I don't open the door and let her in. I'm not ready for that — to grieve the loss of Ledger. I hear conversation in the kitchen. And I need to block their words out.

Taking the envelope in my hands, I open it, pulling out the photos of my husband as a little boy. This is a child I never knew, though — Henry James, a boy whose story is one I've never heard. I search his eyes in each photo, trying to find a clue, desperate to understand the man I gave my life to.

His eyes are sad, and so are mine. I trace my fingertip over the lines of his childlike face, standing in front of houses I've never seen, at a park he's never mentioned. At the beach in swim trunks and a big smile, running toward the break. In the photo, he is running away — is that how it's always been?

Eventually, the house goes quiet and I tuck the pictures back in the envelope, feeling less steady than ever. I stand from the bathroom floor and walk into the hallway; the house is still, empty. Jack and Emma must have left, along with Bethany.

I walk to my bedroom, pull the blankets over me and exhale. It's hot outside but I'm shivering, like I've been plunged in cold water, memories of my life with Ledger covering my body like a dry riverbed filling up after a rainstorm. I let them drown me. Wash me away.

When I was pregnant, Ledger took me to the waterfront. It was a hot day, like it is now. We went to a beach called Point No Point — it felt like the tip of the world. There was so much blue, so much sky, real sand that I could sink my swollen feet into. He brought a kite and it got twisted up in the driftwood and I teased him for not knowing how to fly it properly.

I close my eyes, returning to that day. We spread out on beach towels, my pregnant belly bare in my bikini. I was so brave at twenty, didn't have stretch marks or insecurities like I do now, five years later. Ledger pressed his palm to my stomach when it began to move, and he laughed, shocked and amazed. Our eyes met and it was love. That moment. So much love. He felt it, I know he did. What we shared wasn't pretend. It was as real as anything.

He wouldn't have left me.

We stayed on our towels that day until the tide rolled in.

"I wish we could stay here forever," he said, tucking my wild hair behind my ear. "Just like this."

I rested my head in the crook of his arm. "We'd get washed out to sea."

Now though, I remember how Ledger tensed at that, kissing my forehead. "Would that be the worst thing? To disappear?"

At the time I chalked it up to his childhood in foster care. No family, no friends. Me? I had my coworkers at the diner, my mom who meant the world to me. Before we met, he was a kite, blowing in the wind. I was the string, the tether.

At some point, did I stop paying attention? Did that string snap? It's too painful to consider.

I fall asleep, and when I jerk awake, I wipe drool from my face. Hearing the kids in the kitchen with my mom and Jack, Emma, I walk to my bathroom, splash cold water on my face and look at my watch. I slept for five hours. Makes sense, considering I tossed and turned all night.

In the kitchen, I find Mom pulling out a casserole of macaroni and cheese. Emma is tossing a Caesar salad. Jack's on the floor with the kids, playing with Legos. I try not to bristle at the fact my house is full, that Emma, a woman I hardly know, is still here — but then I hate myself for thinking that. She must feel as torn up by the news about my husband as I am.

"What's all this?" I ask, looking at all the food on the counter. There are Tupperware containers and take-out and Costco meals.

"The neighbors, your customers, people were dropping by all day," Jack says. "Cheryl brought dinner."

"Oh, sweetie," Mom says, wrapping an arm around my shoulder. Kissing my cheek. "You get some good rest?"

"I slept for hours. I can't think of the last time I did that during the day."

"Like you passed out after studying all night for a college exam," Emma says.

I give her a small smile. "I never went to college, actually."

"Really?" She shrugs. "I met Henry in college."

I stiffen again, looking over at my mom. The Ledger I knew never went to college; it's one of the reasons why he struggled to get work. "You guys went to college together?"

"Yeah, Portland State. We met junior year, married my senior year. So I guess I met him after those early years when everyone was learning their limits."

"I didn't know he went to college," I say slowly. "He never said."

Emma's eyes lift. "He hated it, if that's any consolation. I mean, he barely finished his degree." She licks her lips, as if debating what more to say. "He struggled a bit, I mean, with depression."

Mom clears her throat. "Well, the Ledger we knew was very happy," she says tightly, and my heart hurts then, for her words — words that I know she's only saying to protect me. Her loyalty lies with her daughter above all else.

Sure, Mom loved Ledger because I loved Ledger, but she has always had her doubts about him. His track record was messy — lost his job shortly after I got pregnant with the twins. Which I now realize was another lie. He didn't lose it. His employer thought he was dead.

"I'm sure he was happy. How could he not be, with a little girl like Tiny?" Emma says. I back away from the conversation and move to the living room to wrap my kids in hugs.

"You guys have fun with Grandma?"

Clementine smiles. "I jumped in the deep end!"

51

"With a life jacket on," Benny says, holding up a finger to clarify. "And we got ice cream cones. And we watched a movie on her iPad."

"Wow," I say, breathing in the sharp scent of chlorine and loving it because it tells me they had a good day. And right now, they need good. They need sunshine and ice cream and splashing and smiles. They need to believe that their life is not crashing around them, falling apart, into pieces that might never be retrieved. "Sounds like Grandma spoiled you."

"Did Papa call?" Clementine asks.

"Not yet, sweetie," I say just as Mom announces that dinner is ready, that we're eating outside on the patio.

Jack is leaning his back against the edge of the couch, sitting on the floor. "Go wash up," he tells them. They scramble away and he gives me a small smile, squeezing my knee. "You okay?"

While I slept, I had these dreams I can't shake. "Remember Ledger before you got him the job at Grand Slam?"

Jack nods slowly. They met at the auto shop where Ledger was working part-time, finally getting some work. Jack had been coming in all the time for parts as he fixed up an old Challenger. "Why?"

"I just wonder . . . I mean, he was hanging on by a thread back then. Some days he wouldn't get out of bed, could only work part-time because he couldn't get himself together before noon. After that season passed, when he got on antidepressants and got healthy, started working out, and got his CDL, he would never really explain what caused him to spiral so fast. I didn't press him because I didn't want to fight. But what if . . ."

Tears fill my eyes and I bury my face in my hands. "I think I never forced him to tell me because I was too scared of the truth. That he was unhappy because he didn't want this life. This life with me."

Jack pulls me into his arms, and I let out the sobs I've kept contained all day. I know Mom and Emma have the kids outside, and so I take the time I need to cry. Because Ledger is my life and maybe it's a life he never wanted. And if he never wanted it, then what was the point? Five years of a charade where I did everything I could to keep my family together?

Five years when I thought I was fighting for my marriage and my kids and our future. But was I? Or was I fighting to keep a man who wanted to go?

The idea wrecks me, hurts in a way I've never hurt before. Because yes, I had a shitshow of a track record with men before Ledger, but those weren't men who loved me. They weren't men I fell in love with upon first sight. They couldn't hurt me like this because they weren't Ledger Stone.

Henry James.

I pull back from Jack, wiping my face, trying hard to find some shred of truth in my life.

"I loved him," I tell Jack. "But could I have gotten this all wrong?"

My phone rings from the coffee table. I haven't touched it in hours. I answer it, taking the call from Jordan Parrish, the state trooper I spoke with yesterday.

"Mrs. Stone? I have an update."

"Okay," I say, breathless. "And? Did you find him? His body?"

"There have been search and rescue crews on site all day, and as of now, there is still no body recovered, ma'am. We don't believe there is any way he could have survived this crash."

"But maybe you haven't looked everywhere," I say. "Maybe he was swept away in the river and got out somehow and—"

Parrish cuts through. "The most interesting part of discovery is the fact that there was no skidding on the road, no tire marks indicating that this was an accident. Nothing pointing to the possibility that Ledger Stone tried to stop the vehicle."

"So there was no body and you think he meant to go over the guardrail into the gorge?"

Jordan Parrish clears his voice. "Yes, Mrs. Stone. I am calling to tell you that all evidence points to this being a suicide."

53

CHAPTER 11

Every time I roll over, I find Tiny and Benny snuggled closer to me in my bed. I breathe them in, tears flooding my eyes, my body aching with exhaustion. It's the same way I felt when the twins were born.

There were so many sleepless nights, bouncing one baby to sleep, then the next. Pacing the hallway, whispering lullabies that were really my pleas to the universe. Sleep was my only mantra, my single wish.

Ledger wasn't much use. He wasn't a trucker yet, but he was in a dark place. And the anger I felt toward him claws at me now. Too familiar. It wasn't fair that he got to fall apart when I was nursing babies around the clock and changing diapers when other girls my age were celebrating the fact that they were legally able to drink. I never had a rebellious phase — the only wet T-shirt contests I could have entered involved breast milk leaking at inopportune times. Not exactly wild and free.

And I resented the way Ledger rolled over in the bed when I got up out of it to tend to a crying baby. I was angry over the weight of his depression that he carried everywhere he went while I was carrying our newborns.

It wasn't fair to compare — now I know better, am more informed. He wasn't doing anything to hurt me. But that doesn't mean it didn't hurt. Back then, I just knew this: I was twenty-one years old and tied down in a way I never wanted.

And Ledger was sleeping through it all.

The fact he'd done this all before, with another woman, feels like a knife in the heart. It kills me to think that the magic we felt over the newness when the twins were born wasn't the same experience for him that I thought it was.

None of it was new for him.

Eva.

A little girl he never once mentioned.

How can a man not mention his daughter? Not explain her death and the way it shaped him, made him the man he is today?

I hold Tiny in my arms, her sweaty body so sweet, and I kiss her hair, not understanding her father. The man I gave everything to — the man who'd done it all before. If he's alive and is truly on his way to wife number three, will he mention this sweet girl? The daughter who calls him Papa and shares his pine-green eyes? Or will she be as dismissed as Eva? Forgotten. Or long buried. Either way, it breaks my heart.

When I married Ledger, I knew my life was no longer my own. I was pregnant and well aware of the weight of being a mother. My own mom struggled for most of my childhood, not quite reconciling the life she had with the one she wanted.

I don't feel like that, or at least I didn't before I heard about Ledger's accident. I'd put to rest the idea of a carefree life — and I found that motherhood and marriage suited me. It grounded me in a world that had always felt unstable. Ledger and I worked too hard for the life we had to throw it all away.

Didn't we?

Those plans we made, when the twins finally learned to sleep through the night and he finally got well, were so beautiful. Crazy, maybe, considering we were more strapped for cash than ever, and we knew they wouldn't happen for a long time, but they were ours all the same. Dreams carved from the travel books I checked out from the library. Rick Steves' guides on walking across Ireland and backpacking Spain. Ledger lit up when I talked about exploring the world together, a trusty Moleskine journal in my hand, taking notes of our grand adventures. Finally being able to write stories that were bigger than my limited experiences.

"I love it when you get like this," he said one night, the two of us in our bed, the twins tucked in down the hall. The lamp light low, the room fading to black. The two of us finally connecting in the ways I longed for when the twins were smaller.

"Like what?" I asked, closing the book that had lain open in my lap. Setting it on the bedside table, rolling over with my hands on his chest.

"Full of hope." He kissed me, hand on my cheek. "Are you happy now, though, Pen? Is this life enough for you?"

The question hurt him to ask, I know it did. It hurt to answer. But I looked into my husband's eyes and there was no doubt, no faking it, when I answered.

"I love this life we've made. Our twins are literally the cutest things to ever exist. And we're pretty damn cute ourselves."

He smiled, pulling me closer, our legs hooked as tightly as our hearts. Joined together, swearing that nothing would tear us apart.

I close my eyes now, wanting to go back to sleep, the memories as confusing as they are comforting. Rolling over, I hold my little ones as I try to find the solace of sleep. Wanting to dream. Finally, my body listens, and I drift off.

Ledger and I lie on lounge chairs on a white beach, Tiny and Benny laughing in the distance, gentle waves curling at their toes. It's somewhere exotic. Greece? Tahiti? Mazatlán? It's hot. We're sun-drenched and sipping cocktails. Margaritas. Yes. It's Mexico and it's the vacation we never had but always wanted and the kids run up to us, laughing, dragging us into the water, and we all run into the salty waves.

It's wet, water all around my legs, and I wake again, Benny crying. He had an accident, and I help him from the bed. Clementine's still asleep. I run a bath for my little boy, kneeling on the floor, stripping him from his pajamas. I smell coffee, bacon, eggs as I do.

I wash his hair, and he apologizes. "I'm sorry I'm such a baby," he says, and I tell him he's not. That he is my big boy and that I love him so much — so much it hurts.

"I don't want to hurt you," he says.

I say no. "Not that kind of hurt. The kind of hurt that means I'd do anything for you, Benny. The kind of love that is so deep in my belly that it's a part of me. In my skin. My blood. My soul."

Benny looks up at me with those pine-green eyes that match his father's, and it hurts even more. He is Ledger and Ledger is him and where is my husband?

He knows what I'm thinking. "Is Papa coming home today?"

"I don't know, sweetheart," I say, helping him out of the bath and wrapping him in a towel. Then I pick my little boy up off the floor and carry him like a baby burrito past his sleeping sister and into his bedroom. He pulls on underwear. "I'll be a big boy, I promise. No more accidents."

And I blow a raspberry on his belly and tell him I don't care about accidents. I care about him being happy and being safe, and I hug my son. So tight it pushes away the pain of losing Ledger — or who I thought was Ledger — and I hold him.

This little boy who made me a mother was born four minutes before his sister, and when I held him for the first time, I cried. Ledger did too. He was part one of the best thing that ever happened to me, and Clementine was part two, and tears fill my eyes now as I hold Benjamin close. Praying that Ledger comes home, that this was all a mistake.

But what kind of mistake could it be when Emma came to my front porch and Officer Parrish called with news of the accident that wasn't really an accident?

Clementine comes into Benny's room, the one that is painted blue, and she rubs her eyes. "You left me," she says.

"I gave Benny a bath is all." I stand, giving her a morning kiss as Benny pulls on his shorts. And then we follow the scent of bacon into the kitchen and find Emma there, talking with Bethany, who is making breakfast.

"I let Emma in," Bethany says, walking toward me. "She was sitting outside the house in her car, all alone."

"Hope you don't mind," Emma says, reaching for a mug of coffee. Filling it and handing it to me. She is in my house like it's her home, and I want her gone as much as I want her to stay. Everything inside of me is conflicted.

"Hope you don't mind. I needed to do something for you, Pen." Bethany gives me a hug, spatula in hand. "I won't stay long — just let me finish these up and then I'll get out of your hair."

"Where's Thomas?" Benny asks, wondering about Bethany's little boy.

Bethany ruffles his hair. "He's at home with his papa and baby sister."

"My papa is gone," he tells her. "We don't know when he's coming back."

Emma perks up. "Hey, you two, want to watch a cartoon?"

They smile, looking up at me for permission. Grateful that Emma is occupying them, I tell them sure. "Then we'll have breakfast, okay?"

Once the three of them head to the living room, Bethany turns to me. "So, not to be intense, but is there an update? Leo and I are worried sick. The news stopped covering the story."

"Right, because they think it was a suicide," I tell her, unable to meet her gaze.

"What?" Bethany's mouth falls open. "Oh, honey, what in the world?"

I fill her in as quickly as possible, needing the people closest to me to understand — maybe she knows a small bit of information like Jack did about the unknown number.

But when I finish whispering about Emma and Ledger's first marriage and his fake death, she is too stunned to offer a clue if she had one.

And the thing is she doesn't know any secrets. "Ledger loved being a dad, loved you. I would have picked up on it if something were wrong."

"I would have said the same thing, Bethany, but that was before I learned that he was married to Emma. And then that he did this whole thing once before. A car crash from which his body was never recovered. It's eerie, the fact it happened twice."

"So who was the unknown caller?" she asks, swearing as she realizes she's burned a pancake. She tosses it in the trash and turns off the burners.

"No idea. But I call bullshit on all of this."

"All of what?" Bethany opens my drawers and grabs forks, then plates and cups. As far as neighbors go, she's the real deal. We do more than lend a cup of sugar when we're out. We hold the baby while the other stirs the cookie dough. We watch the timer while the other jumps in the shower. We've been at it a year, and I feel like I won the neighbor lottery.

Bethany is eight years older than me — thirty-three and getting her shit together. She has a six-month-old and is still managing to take online classes to get her bachelor's degree. She hasn't had it easy. She had two miscarriages before she had Thomas. They've been bankrupt and almost divorced when Leo had an affair and still, they keep going. Working at it. Looking past their hurt and fighting for the family they both want. It's not perfect — but nothing is. What she and Leo have is real. Messy and flawed — but undoubtedly real.

That's what I thought I had, too.

It's what I still want to find.

"He wouldn't have left me," I say.

"I agree." Bethany sets a jug of orange juice on the counter. "Ledger loves you. Don't let some stranger tell you your story. Figure it out for yourself."

"Just like that?"

Bethany snorts. "I know, easier said than done. But if you want to know the truth, fight for it. Don't let a claims investigator for a corporation tell you what happened to your husband, and don't let some cop you've never met tell you how this all ends. It's your life, Penny. Get the ending you want."

CHAPTER 12

The day is long. I watch hours of Netflix in my bed with the twins, none of us wanting to face the real world. Emma calls at some point and offers to take the twins out. "Or, actually, you keep Benny," she said. "I'll just take Tiny for a mani-pedi."

But I say no. Not only because my four-year-old doesn't need a pedicure, but because I need my children close to me. I wouldn't dare separate them. Especially to spend time with a stranger. Right now they need the familiar. They need me.

If Ledger isn't here to wrap them in a safety net, then I'm the only one who can. And if I'm being perfectly honest, the sharp reality of Ledger and Emma having a child together hurts more than I am ready to admit. Regardless of where Ledger is — dead or alive — he wasn't honest with me while we were married. He wasn't honest about so much.

Jack shows up around noon, delivering sub sandwiches and gifts for the kids.

"This is the new set," Benny says in delight, turning the massive Lego set over in his hands. "It just came out."

"How do you even know that?" I ask, tousling his hair. Benny looks up at me as if I've grown a third eye.

"I saw it online," he says, ripping open the box. Tiny is staring in admiration at the two-foot-tall plastic Disney princess Jack has somehow made magically appear.

"You realize this is better than Christmas? It's kind of problematic," I add with a laugh. "You totally one-upped Ledger and me."

Jack smiles sheepishly. "I figured if there was ever a time to spoil them rotten, this was it."

I run my hands over my arms. "Thanks." The twins scramble to the living room floor to play with their gifts. "We've been kinda immobile today."

"Not too surprised. It's all a lot to take in. I was talking to Jim over at the garage where Ledger used to work. He was all torn up about it. Sends his love to you and the kids."

"That's kind of him. I've been avoiding phone calls, but my mom says everyone is being really kind online. It makes me feel worse though, hearing that. Because Ledger wasn't exactly what I thought he was." I swallow, reaching for the sandwich he bought. Maybe eating something will make me feel better.

We sit down at the kitchen table. Jack grabs a sandwich and begins to unwrap it. "Regardless of this Emma business, he still loved you. And he was still a great dad."

Tears fill my eyes, and I push the food away. "I'm not ready for him to live in the past tense, Jack."

"I get that," he says. "Believe me. I want him to be alive as much as the next guy."

"But?"

Jack swallows, shaking his head. "Dammit, I'm getting a little scared, Penny. They should have found him by now."

"Do you think Emma is stable?" I ask him. "Do you think . . ."

"What I find crazy is that she is so unlike you. How Ledger could go from that to you is . . . usually guys have a type."

I reach for my sandwich, not knowing how to respond. I've been thinking the same thing. "He must have loved her a lot to tell her the truth of his life."

"I don't know what to tell you, Penny," Jack says, his voice strained. "I loved — love — Ledger like a brother. But he didn't treat you the way you deserved."

My jaw tenses at that. "He loves me."

"I know that." Jack pushes his lips forward. "But, Penny, he also left a hell of a lot out."

"You don't have to tell me that," I say, my voice tight, aware of the fact my children are in the living room. "So what do I do?"

"You trust Emma?"

I exhale. "She's been through hell."

"So have you." His eyes meet mine. "I know your childhood was rough. You've said enough for me to understand that before Ledger, the guys you knew weren't the good ones. And you got married because you were pregnant, not because—"

I cut him off, pushing away from the table. "That's too far, Jack. I can't go there yet."

He nods. "I get it. I do. I just see you, a woman with so much talent, who is always talking about wanting to be a writer, do something bigger with your life, and I see Ledger — a guy I care about — not giving you what you want."

"That's simplifying it all too much. Ledger is doing the best he can."

Jack stands and moves to the dishwasher, begins to unload the dishes for me. "If that was the case, then where the hell is he, Penny?" His voice is loud, and his words rattle me, and the way his hands shake as he places coffee mugs in the cupboard, I know they've rattled him too.

I walk toward him, placing my hand on his upper arm, making him stay put. "We're both scared and confused, Jack, but I can't have us fighting. You're the only person in my corner right now who knows Ledger the way I do. My mom never liked him. Emma is on a manhunt. Grand Slam wants to brush this all aside. We have to stick together."

He pulls me to him, and I wrap my arms around his neck. Wanting something steady to hold onto when everything else feels like it's spiraling out of control.

"You're right," he tells me. "We'll find him, Penny. We will."

When we step back, I feel a fresh wave of hope. This isn't the end. The story isn't over. Ledger is out there, and he needs us.

The kids run over to the table, suddenly starved, and I help them get lunch while Jack does a load of dishes. Mom calls to check in on me. The rest of the day passes in a blur.

By bedtime, I'm exhausted — emotionally and physically. When I tuck the kids into their own beds, Tiny looks up at me with such sad eyes.

"What is it, baby?"

Her little chin quivers. "I miss Papa."

I kiss her forehead. "Oh, baby, so do I." I wish I had something more to tell her, something concrete about her father, where he is — if he will ever be home. But I don't and I realize it's not enough. I need more. Need to understand. Bethany's words from this morning roll over in my mind: *It's your life, Penny. Get the ending you want.*

I don't even know what ending I want right now, but this isn't it. If it was truly suicide, wouldn't there be some piece of him left? His body, or at least traces of it, would have been found by now. Yet Jordan Parrish assured me there isn't a single indication that his body is anywhere. Unless he is farther down the river than they think.

I kiss Tiny's and Benny's heads, then turn on their night lights, keeping their doors open a crack.

Then I go to the kitchen and empty the bag from the box of white wine. As I shove the cardboard in the recycling bin, there's a knock on the door. My heart jumps. For a moment, I hold onto hope that it's Ledger.

But he wouldn't knock. Before I question who else might be visiting me at this hour, Bethany pops her head in the door. "Pen? Can I come in?"

I exhale, realizing I'm relieved that it isn't Emma or Jack or anyone else who might need me emotionally in ways I can't give right now. But Bethany doesn't need anything from me — she holds a bottle of white wine and a box of cookies.

"I'm so happy to see you."

"Yeah?" She lifts an eyebrow.

I laugh. "Yeah, this was the last glass in the house, so it looks like the wine fairy arrived just in time."

"It's like I know you or something." She gives me a hug and I squeeze her, grateful for a shoulder tonight. "Oww, not too tight. My boobs are killing me today. Is it just Neva or did your twins go through a biting phase?"

"Oh, sorry," I cringe. "Yeah, Benny was as sweet as a lamb when he nursed, but Tiny was a monster. Still is."

Bethany laughs and I grab her a Mason jar. She pours herself a glass of wine and then tops mine off. We head to the front porch, sitting on the steps. "Tiny is not a monster," she says. "She's literally the cutest preschooler I've ever seen."

I drop my face into my hands, feeling an inch away from completely falling apart. "She's going to be so wrecked if Ledger . . ."

Bethany squeezes my knee. "Oh, Pen. You all will be. But it's still early, right?"

I rip open the cookies and break one in half. "Technically. Yeah. But the whole Emma thing . . . It's just weird, right?"

"It is weird. I just can't picture Ledger lying. He is so . . ."

"Honest?"

Bethany nods. "Yeah, I mean, you know Joanne and Marty?"

I look down the street to their house. Marty bought a boat last year. And Joanne got a tummy tuck. It was a big deal at the time because no one else on the street splurged like that. We were a row of coupon clippers and blue-light-special shoppers. But now it makes more sense. It was their last-ditch effort at happiness.

"Everyone knows Joanne slept with the track coach. And Marty? He was pushing her to lose weight for years. Total creep. So seeing their life fall apart, I get it. Everyone saw it coming. But you and Ledger?" Bethany blinks back tears. "If he lied about everything, there's no hope for any of us."

"What do you mean?" I ask as Leo walks across the grass.

"God, Beth," he huffs. "Neva's been screaming for fifteen minutes, can't you hear her?"

I press my lips together as Bethany exhales loudly. "You're the father, you get that, right?" she asks him, not using a filter on my account. "I'm talking with Penny, it's kind of more important."

Leo grunts. "More important than your newborn?"

I take a long swig of the wine, not wanting to meet either of their eyes. There's nothing more awkward than couples fighting in front of other people — no matter how good of friends you might be.

"She's not a newborn, and I'm trying to sleep train her."

"By ignoring her?"

"Oh my God, you are impossible." She stands, rolling her eyes and then draining her glass of wine. "Love you, Pen. If you need me, you know where to find me. I'll just be chained to the couch with a biting baby strapped to my chest."

"Love you," I say, watching the two of them march off, still bickering. I know Leo has chronic back pain, and I know he has a rough time working as an electrician — but Bethany is juggling so much while he's at work. Would it kill him to give her a break?

I take another sip of wine, watching them enter their house, the television screen brightening their living room. Leo plops down in the recliner and I look away, wishing they had blinds. I know they argue sometimes, but that seemed uncalled for on so many levels.

Wiping the cookie crumbs from my lap, I stand, walking back inside. I pour myself another glass of wine, wondering just how much we know about anyone. Our best friends. Our husbands.

After shoving the cork back into the bottle, I walk into the living room. My eyes land on the one thing I haven't dared crack open since I learned of the accident. Ledger's laptop.

My mom gave him this laptop a few years ago when she upgraded. He didn't spend too much time on it, never having a computer before then as far as I knew. Then again, the Ledger I knew barely graduated high school after growing up in foster care, then worked at an auto shop until he got the service training job. He worked there a few years before meeting me. I didn't ask for more details. I never once asked, *Did you have another wife during this time?* Or, *Were you ever in a car accident that led to the faking of your death?* It's not the sort of thing that comes up.

Instead, those few times we were together before I found out I was pregnant, we focused on our wants, our dreams, our desires. Sex, for one. But also, a future filled with travel and spontaneity. He wanted to shake himself out of the monotony of the life he was living, going from one auto dealership to the next. He wondered if there was more.

I remember laughing, feeding him peach pie by the forkful after the diner closed for the night. "We could go," I told him. "Leave it all behind."

Even after the pregnancy, we thought we might leave. Travel the world with a baby strapped to our back. Take our meager savings and make a go of it. Then I went in for my twenty-week ultrasound and there were two babies and we knew the plan would have to change.

But somehow, even though it was never my first choice, our life together became the only thing that mattered. This new reality became our dream. Our babies were growing and our love at first sight was becoming something more permanent. And somehow, this new life we'd been given became big enough for us both.

And now as I open his laptop, sitting at the kitchen table, the sliding glass door open, letting in the breeze from the August night, I wonder if it ever was big enough for Ledger. I turn on the laptop, wondering what else I might learn. What else my husband kept from me.

Another woman, sure. Maybe bank accounts he had hidden. Criminal charges. Illegitimate children. I have literally no idea.

As I'm prompted to enter the password, I enter Penny4URthoughts. Immediately, I'm directed to his desktop.

His password is what it always was and I exhale, having held in a breath for far too long. Maybe Ledger is still my Ledger. Maybe this has all been a stupid misunderstanding. Maybe.

The photo on his desktop is of Benjamin and Clementine, at the county fair, on the carousel. They are riding ponies, smiling so wide. Holding on so tight.

Neatly organized on the side of the screen are two folders. 'FAMILY PHOTOS' and 'TRUCK MAINTENANCE INFORMATION TO BE GIVEN TO GRAND SLAM'.

I'm tempted to go down his family photo vortex. My heart wants to spiral out in the memories that will take the sharp edges off my emotions — but I don't. Because they might not soften this blow. Seeing our family might trigger something I can't undo. I would start clicking through images and end up in a heap of tears, sobbing so loud I'd wake the kids. And then I'd accidentally explain the truth to them: Your papa might never come back.

So I refrain from the indulgence. Tonight I don't need that anyways. Tonight I need to fight for the ending I want.

I open the second folder, and I start reading. Relieved, I take a sip of wine.

This is what I was looking for.

* * *

When Cheryl calls from the diner the next morning, I pick up, knowing I owe her a check-in. She was with me when I learned about Ledger's accident, so she deserves a follow-up. I give her a brief rundown, that his body hasn't been found and there's nothing conclusive at this time. I don't say Officer Parrish called it a suicide.

"So you think maybe . . . maybe he's still with us?"

I swallow, not wanting to tell her any information that could bite me in the ass. I love Cheryl, I do, but she runs Over Easy and knows the entire town from serving them hash browns and burned coffee for the last twenty years.

"I'm holding out hope, Cheryl. Maybe it's crazy to think he may still be alive, but I'm praying for a miracle."

My words sound sweeter and more sincere than I feel right now. Truth is, dead or alive, he lied to me. About so much.

And yes, I want him back — but more than that, I want to figure out who my husband really is. Who is Ledger Stone? Who was Henry James? And is he out there right now creating a third identity?

"I think I'll come into work tomorrow," I tell Cheryl. "I need the cash."

"Oh, sweetheart, you can't work. You're a mess."

"I'm not," I say, blowing my nose.

"Well, you can call it what you like, but this whole town is worried sick for you. You'd be overrun with questions. And darlin', I don't think you have all the answers quite yet."

I hang up, knowing she's probably right. Customers would be peppering me for information all day long and I can hardly look my kids in the eye right now, let alone the regulars at Over Easy.

Still, I know my checking account balance. Rent is due in a week, along with all our other bills. And Grand Slam put a hold on the payment they owe Ledger, and without life insurance, we need some kind of income to stay afloat.

I need to go talk to Grand Slam again. Mom agrees to take the kids for the day again, so I load them up and take them to the apartment complex. Mom snuffs out her cigarette as I walk into her place, and she asks for an update.

"We hibernated all day yesterday," I say as the kids run circles in her small living room.

"I made you muffins," Mom calls. They swoop into the kitchen, swiping them from the cooling rack.

"Hey, sit at the table, you two," I tell them.

"So you stayed home?" she asks me once the kids are settled with food.

I pour myself a glass of iced tea and sit down on her sofa, next to her. "Yeah, we watched every episode of *Ninjago* on Netflix. I'm Sensei Woo'd out, but the kids—" I turn to them, and as if on cue, they give karate chops in the air. Mom laughs, clapping for her grandchildren as if they've truly mastered something.

"And Emma, is she still around?" she asks.

I nod. "Yeah. I think she's hoping Ledger miraculously shows up so she can kick his butt. She's pissed." I remember the look on her face when she flipped through our family photo albums. All those memories she felt personally robbed of. And I understand why.

"You trust her?"

I swallow. "They had a daughter."

Mom covers her mouth. "Oh, Penny."

I pull my fingers through my thick hair, looking up at the ceiling. "I should be heartbroken — their daughter died when she was an infant. But the main emotion I have is anger. He lied about so much."

"I can't believe they had a child together. Why would he lie about everything?"

I shake my head, at a loss. "I feel like I'm betraying him to doubt his love for me . . . but everything is stacking up against him."

"You aren't betraying him." Mom shakes her head in shock. "I just can't believe he had a child."

"Me neither." I press my lips together, leaning closer, not wanting the kids to overhear. "I know you never liked him, Mom." I lift my hand to stop her from interrupting. "And I want to believe that he's the man I thought he was . . . but . . . poor Emma. She thought the man she loved was killed. I feel terrible for her. Any hope of moving on died the moment she found out her husband was alive."

"How do you recover from that?" Mom asks, not expecting an answer.

"It's weird," I say. "Before this, what I wanted was a life exciting enough to have a story to tell, something to write about. But now that this has happened, all I want is normal. I just want Ledger back."

Mom pulls me into a hug as tears fall down my cheeks. The twins notice and bound over to the sofa, piling on me.

"Bear hug," Benny says. They're the words Ledger uses when he tackles the twins to the ground.

"Bear hug," I repeat, pulling them close, Tiny's hand on my neck, Benny crawling up my back. "We're gonna be okay," I say to them as much as to myself. We have to be — we're all we've got.

I give them kisses and another round of hugs before I go.

"You going to be okay driving?" Mom asks.

I nod. "The drive will be good, it will give me a chance to clear my head. I'm not looking forward to this chat with Grand Slam. But I need to see why they put a stop to payment on his paycheck."

"Did Ledger have life insurance?"

I shake my head. "No. We meant to get it, but we never got around to it."

Mom nods. "If it's a suicide," she whispers, "you won't get a cent from a settlement."

My shoulders stiffen. "I know."

CHAPTER 13

The corporate offices for Grand Slam Transit are in downtown Tacoma, about forty-five minutes from our town of Riverport. I blast the radio the entire drive, the windows of the minivan rolled down since the AC busted a week ago. It was another item on the honey-do list for Ledger when he got back from this trip. Except he never made it home.

Sun shines bright and as I cross the Narrows Bridge, rays of light turn the Sound into a blanket of blue glitter. My phone is on silent and I lose myself in the pop music. By the time I pull into the parking lot, my unruly hair is windblown and my vitamin D is boosted.

Checking in at security is more formal than I expect. I go through a metal detector, then sign in at a welcome desk.

"I'm here to see Vance Donovan," I say.

Donning a visitor badge, I head up the elevator, and Vance Donovan is waiting for me when I step out onto the third floor.

"Mrs. Stone, so glad you could come in." He greets me warmly enough, but his face is drawn in a frown, his coloring gray and worn. "I can only imagine what a hard time this has been for you."

In his office, he pulls out a file and clears his throat, scanning the file in front of him as if trying to remember just who my husband was. He's never met Ledger, knows nothing about him.

Ledger isn't a big deal at the company; he drives one of their trucks, which is a pretty routine job as far as long-haul trucking goes. He leaves for two weeks at a time, comes home for three days, leaves again. He doesn't have an office, of course, but he has the back of his cab. He outfits it with his gear — sleeping bag, cooler, iPad — and in order to save on costs, he sleeps in his truck most of the year.

I watch him, this forty-year-old man in his cheap suit, working an office job that is mundane at best. At least the diner has big windows, letting the sunlight in, the rainclouds rolling by. Different customers every hour, always someone wanting to strike up a conversation, lots of opportunity to make someone's day better. Brighter. It's one of the reasons I'm still there. If I can't be in Europe or South America, backpacking or driving an RV across the country, at least I have a chance to make the people around me smile over a cup of coffee and a slice of pie.

"I have a few questions," I start.

Vance sucks in air between his teeth. "Well, that makes two of us."

"First off," I say, already bristling, "why is there a stop payment on his last paycheck? We need that money."

Vance lifts his hands in defense. "Fair enough, but the fine print of his contract states there will be a stop payment if there is question about the safety of the driver. And considering everything we know about Mr. Stone, there are plenty of red flags for our legal team to keep this wrapped up for quite a while."

"Red flags like what?" I ask. "You mean the lack of tire marks? Because you aren't looking at this from every angle."

Vance raises his eyebrows as I pull out a manila envelope from my purse. I spent last night printing off every document in Ledger's file.

I push the envelope toward him and sit back. "My husband had concerns about the brake system on the Grand

Slam trucks for quite a while," I say as Vance pulls out the papers. There are lines circled in red, arrows pointing to auto parts in the photos, and official words like "tampered" and "intentional" have been highlighted. "Ledger raised these concerns to the safety board — I printed the emails here. And he took photographs of the reason he believed the maintenance with the trucks wasn't up to par."

Vance scans the documents. The documents where Ledger took detailed notes of the maintenance schedule, the worn tire treads, the oil left unchanged, the brake issues that needed to be addressed.

"This is all quite interesting, Mrs. Stone, but it does nothing to change the facts."

I scoff. "Of course it does. It changes everything. Ledger didn't kill himself. The brakes went out. He died senselessly. At the hands of Grand Slam, which refused to take his concerns seriously."

Vance clasps his hands together, elbows on his desk. "I wish that were the case, Mrs. Stone, and I can only imagine how hard this must be for you. If you'd like to speak with someone in HR—"

"No. I want to talk to you, the investigator on this case."

"My hands are tied. I complete the investigation and from there, corporate makes a decision. I'm sorry, but there will be no back pay and no claims to process at this time. I understand this is the worst news I could give you, but the facts speak for themselves."

I usually feel confident, capable, like I can pull myself up by my bootstraps and get the job done, even if it's not a job I want to do. But this is different. Vance is looking at me with pity and I hate it. Hate him. For looking at me like this. Not taking me seriously. Because this is more serious than anything I have ever faced before. My husband's integrity is on the line.

And yes, there is a hell of a lot that I'm confused about — Emma thinks he's off with wife number three, and I don't know what to believe.

But I do know this — Ledger wouldn't have killed himself. No. It's not possible. We weren't perfect, but we were happy. We were. And I'm not just telling myself a story I want to hear. It's the truth. My truth. And I'm not letting Vance fucking Donovan tell me otherwise.

"No," I say, my fist on his desk. "Those aren't the facts. Grand Slam doesn't want to deal with the truth. And I'll hire a lawyer if that is what's necessary to make the truth known."

Vance shakes his head and opens his own folder, sliding photographs my way of Ledger at a convenience store. "We have the facts, Mrs. Stone. Your husband was on antidepressants, and the night before he killed himself, he bought Benadryl. Doping himself up, putting himself behind the driver's seat, and driving off the side of the road."

"He has allergies," I tell Vance Donovan, seething across the table from him. "He took Benadryl for them. He called me the night before, telling me he was buying it. And as for his depression, fuck you. You can't withhold this investigation because he has a treatable condition that he sees a doctor for."

Vance trills his fingertips on his mahogany desk and I storm out, leaving the office complex furiously. I left copies of my findings with Vance and I told him to figure this out, or I'd be going to the cops.

And I would.

I will.

CHAPTER 14

Driving away from Vance Donovan's office, my hands grip the steering wheel tight. The majestic views of Mount Rainier are as distant as my thoughts. Vance's words brought me back to a time I'd rather forget.

Ledger's depression nearly tore our family apart.

Three years ago, I found myself with one-year-old twins, at my breaking point. It was a place I was familiar with because Ledger had been there for months: broken.

I had been his rock that whole time, and *this* time I couldn't manage alone, yet he still couldn't pick himself off the couch and take a shower and be the person I needed. Nothing about it felt fair.

"He needs to see a doctor," I told my mom as the twins crawled around her carpeted apartment floor. She may not have made safe choices when I was young — there had been a revolving door of abusive men in our home after my father left — but she was a good mom and an amazing grandma.

When Clementine and Benjamin were born, they became her pair of much-needed rose-colored glasses. Her life had been hard, but now, as their grandma, she got a second chance. And she was intent on doing it right.

Sitting on the floor with the babies, we tried to make a plan. It was hard. We weren't the sort of women who saw a problem and dealt with it well. Mom and I took life's blows and never fought back.

But this time, it was different. It wasn't just my asshole high school boyfriends whom I needed to stand up to, or the shitty men who promised Mom forever and then took it out on her when they didn't want to own up.

No. It was different for two reasons. Well, three, really. Because Tiny and Benny needed me to be strong. Ledger did too.

I wouldn't let my family down.

After spending months journaling my feelings of new motherhood, of wearing a smile and a nursing bra, of running ragged as often as I ran loads of laundry, I realized nothing was changing on Ledger's end. It was me, night after sleepless night, trying to keep our family out of the deep end of the pool. I was tired of treading water.

So I reached out for a lifeboat in the form of my mother.

"Will he go see someone?" Mom asked, eyebrows raised, handing Benny a teething biscuit so she could avoid making eye contact with me. Uninterested, he threw it on the floor. I knew Mom was doing her best not to be judgmental. But she never trusted Ledger, even before he became depressed.

She resented the fact this man — this man I loved with all my heart — came between me and my plans for the future. She couldn't understand that yes, my dreams changed when I met Ledger, but that didn't mean I had changed. I was still the same Penny, with pen and paper in hand, attempting to document my small and lovely life.

"I'll force him to talk to a therapist," I said. "This can't be our new normal. You watching the twins while I work as many shifts as possible, living in a one-bedroom apartment and barely getting by. Mom, I don't need everything, but I need more than this." Tears fell down my face and I pulled Tiny to me, needing the comfort of her squishy arms and soft baby smell.

Mom stood and refilled my coffee, splashing in vanilla creamer. Her movements were familiar and welcoming; she was taking care of me, and I needed her to. I felt alone — twenty-two and so far over my head I couldn't breathe.

I had gotten swept up in a whirlwind. Ledger and I had married after we got pregnant with the twins, and for a while it really felt like everything was going to be okay.

Sure, he lost his job, but he was looking for another one, and I had my waitressing shifts at Over Easy. Tips were good, and we could make it. We were living on a prayer, sure, but it was a good one.

Until it wasn't. Until Ledger couldn't find any work, and he was going to Labor Ready in the mornings to barely bring home minimum wage. He was a grown man with an ego that was bruised. And two newborns at home with a wife still wearing thick postpartum pads. He had to make ends meet because if he couldn't, we were screwed.

That had been a year ago. We'd been in a holding pattern for far too long.

And I was tired. So, so tired.

Mom handed the coffee to me. "Oh, sweetheart," she sighed, eyeing her pack of cigarettes. I knew she wanted to smoke. We were both stressed. "You can move in here," she offered. I looked around her two-bedroom apartment. She kept it immaculate. She was always good at housekeeping — she said it was the one thing she had absolute control over.

"We're not going to do that. My paycheck covers almost everything and I'm on WIC and even applied for food stamps." Tears filled my eyes again; I hated to cry over this godsend, but it felt like those dreams I'd had a year or two ago — of seeing the world and being free — were a thousand miles away. Out of reach. Ledger knew it, and Mom knew it, and I knew. And when my kids grew up, they'd know it too, that pipe dreams were just that: buried underground, never to see the light of day.

"I can move into a three-bedroom unit," she said. "I think one is opening up at the end of the month."

"Ledger wouldn't like the five of us all living together. It would feel like we were taking over your life." I pulled Tiny to my chest to let her nurse, my breasts suddenly full from the onslaught of emotion.

"I wasn't meaning all five of you, sweetie. Maybe it's time for Ledger—"

I cut her off. "Mom, no. I love him."

"I know, but, Pen, does that mean you have to be married to him?"

The question stung, and I felt like I had breached something — letting Mom into my marriage like this. Truth was she didn't know anything about my marriage. She compared it to her relationships when really, there was no comparing the two. Ledger would never intentionally hurt me. Whereas the men she dated had left marks that took time to heal.

"This is just a season," I told her firmly. "It's temporary. Ledger needs professional help, and he will get better." I wiped the tears from my eyes. "He has to."

"Or what?" Mom asked softly.

"I don't know, Mom. I'm in over my head. I love him, I do, but it's hard."

"I wish I could tell you everything was going to be okay, but I can't promise that. I stayed with your father for longer than I should have, and I kept going with plenty more men who had outstayed their welcome."

"Ledger is different than those guys, Mom. I know you don't believe me, think he is no good for me, but—"

Now it was Mom's turn to cut me off. "No, I didn't say he was no good for you. I've said I'm sad that being with him has meant letting all your dreams die."

"I have new dreams, Mom. Why can't that be enough for you?"

Mom's eyes reached mine. "The question is, is it enough for you?"

I didn't know how to answer. Because the truth was too painful to put words to. If my marriage was going to continue just as it was, then no, it wasn't enough. I needed a partner who was strong enough to stand by my side. And right now, Ledger couldn't stand at all.

"What do you think triggered it?" she asked. "This spiral?"

I swallowed, looking at the twins and knowing that once they were born, everything had gone downhill. I remember so clearly what I told her then, the words coming back to me as I drive home. "It's like he is grieving something," I had told my mom. "Like something or someone died. But I don't know who or what."

She placated me the best she could, could see how torn up I already was and decided to back off. Said that the man Ledger was before kids is gone. How some men struggle with the responsibility. The changing role.

But now I see that wasn't what was happening.

Ledger had been through all this before, had been a father, a husband. And he had walked away from all of it. Why?

I came home from my mother's that day and gave my husband of eighteen months an ultimatum: Go to a psychiatrist or leave and never come back.

My words snapped something in him. He got up from the couch and showered and left the house for six hours, and when he came home, he had a prescription for Zoloft and an appointment card with a counselor for the next week. And every week after.

He took the pills and apologized until I believed him and went to therapy and got a part-time job at an auto shop. He met Jack and took the training classes for his CDL and he got hired with Grand Slam Transit, and we got our three-bedroom rental house with a back yard and a BBQ.

It wasn't easy. Ledger worked hard. We both learned what depression was, how it felt like a thick blanket wrapped around him and how just pulling it down, away from his eyes, felt like a massive undertaking. I found ways to back off, and he found ways to step up. We found a new rhythm, one I didn't anticipate needing, but the tempo of our life had changed with the arrival of the twins.

This new chapter wasn't easy for either of us. But we made it work. I left for a coffee shop on Sunday mornings while he watched football. I would take my laptop and type out stories, revising the same paragraph for hours and loving every minute of it. Ledger learned that fatherhood suited him in the way being a mom suited me. We were both the right level of relaxed versus crazed. We weren't helicoptering them, but we were quick to run interference.

After a particularly dramatic morning at the park, we would dissect the mommies and their babies — claiming we would never be so hypervigilant, but then the moment Benny or Tiny fell, we would swoop in and coddle them. We would laugh about it later, commiserating in the way all new parents can. It stopped being about me desperately trying to keep the family together and became all of us being in that battle together. We were winning.

All that information tells me that now, considering the thriving life we shared, there is literally no way Ledger would kill himself. No way, never.

But as I cross the bridge toward home, my heart pounds. I finally realize what Ledger's depression was about.

It felt like someone had died because someone *had*.

Henry James had died. The man my husband was. A man who went to college and had a job, a career, a wife, a house with a picket fence — and then he met me and knocked me up and we were living in seven hundred square feet, counting our change to buy diapers.

Of course he became depressed.

He had killed himself. Or at least, let the man he once was die.

The question I have now is: Why would he want to do that all over again?

CHAPTER 15

The morning after my disastrous meeting with Vance Donovan, I try to focus on the kids. Not the fact that my checking account is nearing a dangerous new low with no cash flow on the way. For a moment, I reconsider getting a shift at the diner, but Cheryl is right — the story about Ledger is out, and the diner doesn't need me around to kill business.

Mom called late last night. She'd been out at the bar and heard some folks talking about Ledger, how he'd killed himself and how his widow won't see a cent from Grand Slam. The thought of strangers discussing my husband like that caused me to sink into the couch, my life reaching a new low.

"I was wondering, though," she said. "Should we start thinking about a service?"

Anger rose up in me at her words. "No. There's not even a body. I'm not even considering that now."

She apologized profusely as I ended the call. Crawling into bed, I slept like a rock, the twins snuggled close to me. Exhaustion overtook me in a way I had never known before.

When I wake, I push all thoughts of the future and the past away and focus solely on the present: on my children.

It's a hot day, hitting the high eighties, and as I pull my thick locks into a hair-tie, I think about how I can make this another normal summer day for them.

I crank all the fans in the house on high and we make homemade playdough together, just me and the twins. That is what we need right now — normal. Of course, just as the mixer is kneading the cornstarch and water together, the doorbell rings.

"Don't touch the food coloring," I warn their little hands as I head to the front door. Emma is here, in a starched white collared tank top and capris, her hair looking expertly styled.

"Were you just at the salon?" I can't help but blurt out.

Emma bristles. "Yes, I was, actually."

My mind is on the conversation I had earlier with my mom — her suggestion that we have a service for Ledger — and standing here now, confronted with Emma, I feel a surge of annoyance at her hanging around. Yes, I know she's twisted into my family tree in a bizarre way, but right now, I just want my family close. No one else.

"Look, I know you are invested in Ledger—"

"Henry, you mean," she says, cutting me off. Her lips purse, words tight.

It's the way she says it, so sharp, so matter-of-fact, that puts me on edge. "What are you still doing in town, Emma? I know you want to find answers, but right now, I just want to grieve."

"So you think he's actually dead?"

"I don't know what I think," I say, suddenly exhausted. "I just know the man I loved may never return, not in the way I remember him. And that breaks my heart."

"I don't get it," she says, shaking her head. "I'm trying to be a good friend to you and help you and everything. But it's not good enough. I'm so sorry." She wipes the tears from her eyes. "I just wanted to help."

I groan, pushing back my hair, guilt inching its way up my spine. "Look, I'm not pushing you away. I'm just trying to understand what you hope to find."

Her eyes spill over with tears. "I want to find my husband."

Benny calls for me from the kitchen. "Mama, it's all mixed."

Emma meets my eyes. "I'm sorry. You have the kids. I shouldn't barge in. It's just . . . You're the only one who understands."

"Understands what?"

"How much I loved him."

It's painful to watch another woman grieve the man who you thought was yours and yours alone. It's not a feeling I'd wish on anyone. I certainly don't wish it on Emma.

"Look, I'm spending time with the kids right now. But come back later, for dinner. Okay?"

"You sure?"

I nod. "Yeah. You're not alone, Emma. Okay? We will figure this out together." I give her a hug that isn't warm, exactly, but my heart has thawed toward her in an unexpected way. She looks like she's going to blow over, and maybe in the middle of this mess, I can be something solid to hold onto.

Back in the kitchen, I divide the balls of dough between the three of us, adding droplets of dye to each one. Pink for Tiny. Green for Benny. Blue for me. We knead it until it's soft and warm in our hands, forming shapes. I make a heart and Tiny makes an X and an O. "Grandma says that means hugs and kisses."

I lean over, showering them with both. I breathe them in, the salty tang of the dough in the air, the possibility of shaping something new from the wreckage of our life with our fingertips.

Later, just as we are cleaning up the playdough, my mom calls and I put her on speakerphone, wanting her to hear how happy the kids are. Focus on them, I think, not the clusterfuck that is my personal life. That is their father. Mom tells them they can come over for a sleepover soon, then she ends the call.

"You two clean up the playdough and then once I switch the laundry, I'll put on the sprinkler for you in the backyard, okay?"

I load the dryer, smiling at their giggles and wishing Ledger were here to hear them. He's not coming back, though, as much as I keep hoping he will . . . The more time that passes, the more unrealistic it becomes.

As I add a dryer sheet to the load, I decide that I should go to the site of the accident. I need closure, one way or another. Mom will think the idea of me going out there is insane, a cruel punishment, but I need to see the crash site. To understand.

But as I load the washer, the machine doesn't seem to like my plans. Water begins to pour from the hose in the back, flooding the floor in seconds. "Oh, shit," I groan, reaching to turn the machine off.

I rush to the garage to turn off the water and yell at the kids, telling them to stay put. It takes me several minutes to find the valve and when I do, my eyes are burning with frustration. I needed a nice, normal day. Not this.

When I get back to the laundry room, just off the kitchen, I see Jack is here, iced coffees in hand. "Hey," I say, breathless. "When did you get here?" I see Tiny and Benny bound from their bedroom, already suited up for the promised sprinkler.

"Just walked in the door. You must not have heard. What's going on?" he asks, scanning the floor where water is seeping across the linoleum.

"The washer busted." I mop my forehead with the back of my hand. "Shit timing. This is not what I want to deal with."

"Let me look at it, okay?"

I nod numbly, placing dirty towels on the floor to sop up the water, my shoulders falling. Grateful for Jack but wanting my husband.

Jack pulls out the washer, unplugging it as he cleans up the water.

"Why don't you take the kids out, to the park down-town? The one with that water zone?" he says. "Let me sit here and mess with this."

"You sure?"

He squeezes my shoulders. "Penny, you should go get some fresh air."

I shake my head. "I don't want to deal with people."

"Wear sunglasses and a large hat." He hands me the iced latte. "Go."

"Emma was coming over later," I say. "But I don't want to deal with her. Can you get her to back off?"

Jack frowns. "What happened?"

I shake my head. "Kids, why don't you go wait outside? I'll be there in a sec, okay?" I look back to Jack. "Look, nothing happened, but I still want to believe the best with Ledger and she—"

Jack cuts me off. "You think he's alive? That he wants to come back to you?"

I swallow, offended. "Yeah. I do."

He runs a hand over his jaw. "Penny, doesn't it look sketchy, the whole thing?"

"What are you saying?"

Jack looks me in the eyes. "I'm saying Ledger's story doesn't add up. He lied to you for five years and you're still hoping he'll come back. Choose you. But you need to face the facts, Penny. He's gone. And either he died from faulty brakes, or he killed himself, or he left you the same way he left wife number one."

I slap him then.

My hand crosses that fine, chiseled jaw of his and lands square on his cheek. The shocking sound echoes through the house. My fingertips are hot and his eyes are bruised. "I'm sorry," I say, shocking even myself. "I can't believe I did that, I'm so sorry, Jack." Tears blur my vision and I shake my head, but Jack takes hold of my wrists.

"Don't apologize, Penny. I should have kept my fucking mouth shut. But shit, Pen, I hate this. I fucking hate this for you of all people, Penny. The best woman I've ever fucking known, a woman Ledger would be crazy to leave, and I'm pissed at him for you, the kids — all of it." Jack's crying now too and I wrap my arms around him. He holds me and I hold him and we cry.

Cry the tears I refused to shed in front of Vance Donovan, tears I bottled up last night, going numb instead

86

of weak in the knees, after Mom called telling me what everyone was saying. But now I let the emotions pour out of me.

I can hear Bethany in the front yard talking with the kids, and then I see her in my doorway tiptoeing in quietly, and I pull back from Jack, wiping my eyes; he wipes his too.

"Oh, sorry, Pen," she says. "I don't mean to intrude. But I saw the kids outside, they said they were going to the splash pad park but—" Her eyes take in the mess of water on the floor. "Well, your day's just getting worse, isn't it? Look, I was going crazy at home anyways. Why don't I take the twins to the park with my kids and you can breathe, have a moment alone?" She looks at Jack, then me. "Or, you know, with Jack."

"Jack's just here to fix the washer."

His eyes meet mine and I know I've hurt him. He's not here for the washer. Deep down, I know he is here for me. And I don't know what to do with that. I don't want Jack to think I'm holding some flame for him — I'm not. I never have.

But I don't want to push Ledger's closest friend away either. It's not like he's done anything inappropriate. He brought me coffee and is fixing my washing machine. He is crying and broken and mad at Ledger the same way I am.

"Actually, I'm exhausted." I run my fingers over my temples. "I have a crazy headache, and even though I slept like a rock last night, I feel like I could sleep all day." The thought of driving two hours to the site where Ledger's truck went into the river seems insane. No way can I make the drive in this worn-down state.

"I'm just gonna take the twins," Bethany says. "We'll be back in a few hours."

"Really?"

She nods. "Of course, babe."

I pack a bag for the twins, kissing them goodbye, and Jack grabs a toolbox from his truck. The kids are gone, he's occupied, and my eyes land on Ledger's laptop.

When I started digging last night, I found the information I needed for Vance Donovan.

Maybe if I start looking deeper, this time I'll find the information I'm looking for.

CHAPTER 16

I take the iced coffee, the computer charger and Ledger's laptop and head to my bedroom. Jack can handle a washing machine crisis, and he already has his tools spread out on the floor.

Knowing the kids are safe when they're with Bethany, I take advantage of the quiet house, this early afternoon reprieve. I need to learn more about how this all began, and I can't do that with Tiny and Benny around, needing my attention.

I close my door, kicking off my flip-flops, and face the fan toward me; the house is a furnace and there's no breeze to help with the heat. But the iced coffee is delicious. I take a sip. I adjust the pillows on the mattress that's shoved against the wall, my bedroom a rumpled mess, and I lie there for an hour, lost in my thoughts. Wondering where my husband is. Why he'd leave. Refusing to admit that he might simply be dead.

Sweat runs between my breasts, and I have an urge to strip myself and take a quick shower. In the bathroom, I pull off my cut-off shorts, my tank top. I slip from my underwear and bra and step into the cool shower. My scalp tingles in pleasure as I pull the hair-tie out and run my fingers through my locks.

Leaning against the tile, I let myself sink to the floor. My body is a knot of tension, and I pretend I'm at a spa, like the one I went to for my birthday last year. Ledger surprised me with a gift card to a day spa a few towns over. I got a professional massage — the first in my life. Afterwards, I was given a fluffy bathrobe and spent an hour in the steam room, the sauna, the showers that had fancy buttons to adjust the water pressure.

It's not the same here, in my overheated house with a husband who may or may not be gone. I'm not relaxed like I was that day, when I left the spa with an actual glow to my skin. Feeling decadent, and a little shocked. I couldn't believe Ledger had spent so much money on that kind of unnecessary indulgence, but the week before my birthday had been rough, and that gift was Ledger doing his very best to make me happy.

I'd been upset — jealous, actually — after seeing Julia, an old friend from high school, on Instagram posting photos about her trip to France. Versailles and the Louvre and cafes, sipping wine, with captions like *#LivingMyBestLife #RoseAllDay* and *#EarnedThis #WorkHardPlayHard*. I hated her. For thinking that her hard work got her there. Because I was working my ass off at the diner and I had burned my arm on the grill that morning and it hurt like hell. Hurt to think that clearing tables and pouring coffee would never get me there, to the Mona Lisa and the Arc de Triomphe. I hated that it hurt so bad. Not having that.

Putting the kids to bed that night, so many months ago, I tripped over Walmart toys, the plastic arms of Barbie dolls jamming into my bare feet. I swore under my breath as I walked into the hall, baskets of dirty laundry sitting there for how many days, dishes in the sink from breakfast, lunch and dinner. Ledger whistling in the garage as he worked on his car.

I remember getting so mad, slamming the cupboards, the dishwasher, exaggerating my sighs, my groans, until Ledger came out of the garage, into the house, asking me what my deal was.

"Nothing." I pursed my lips. Crossed my arms.

He took me by the hips, pulling me to him, kissing my neck, and I instinctively whimpered in pleasure. I wanted to fight, to shout, to vent about what my life wasn't. How it wasn't fair. But Ledger didn't want to argue.

He smelled like gasoline and sweat. I wanted him. Wanted him to make the hurt go away, and when he kissed me firmly on the lips, tears fell down my cheeks and my shoulders shook, and he took my face in his hands.

"What's going on, Penny?"

How do you tell the man you love, the man who has been there for you through thick and thin, whom you've been through the trenches with, that this life, this beautiful messy broken life, isn't enough?

You can't. Because I loved Ledger and knew he'd been in the garage after being on the road for three weeks. He'd been home two days and was doing something fun, in the fucking garage, for the first time since he got back. And I wanted that for him. For him to get a break.

I didn't want him to do the dishes and clean the house, but I didn't want to either. I wanted to be in Paris and I wanted to eat expensive gelato and walk down the Seine. I was twenty-four years old, so close to twenty-five, and I thought it would never, ever happen, never change. That this was it.

And the part that shamed me was the idea that this — this beautiful life, a man who loved me and two children who were happy and healthy and a home of our very own — wasn't enough. Because who the hell did I think I was? I didn't want to be Julia. I wanted this.

But sometimes, like that day, it didn't feel like it was enough.

Ledger held my face and asked me again what was wrong and this time I found words. "I'm just tired and I'm glad you're home."

And I was. Tired and happy and his.

"What else?" he asked, his eyes on mine, thumbs wiping away the tears. He picked me up and set me down on the counter. My hands ran over his solid chest. I could tell him the truth. My fears. He was the love of my goddamn life. If I couldn't be honest with him, how could I be honest with myself?

"Sometimes I just wonder, Ledger, if this is it."

His lips pulled into a half smile, threading his fingers through my wild hair. "Nah," he said, his forehead pressing against my own. "Penny, there's a whole world out there, waiting for you. For us. We'll get there. I promise."

"How?" I asked. We'd talked about me going to college once the twins were in school and maybe I could. It was only two years away. I didn't even know what I'd want to do. I never gave myself permission to think beyond getting out of Riverport.

"I know I've let you down in lots of ways, and I hate that, babe. Because I fucking love you."

"Don't apologize," I said, not wanting to relive his breakdown. We'd recovered. We were stronger than ever. I didn't begrudge him a thing, because I knew what didn't kill us made us stronger. I believed that. I still do.

"I know we can't pack up and go tomorrow. Hell, we don't even have passports," he said, his voice low and gravelly. "But I know one day you will be able to do all the things you want."

"I don't want much."

"You want Paris," he said with a smile, as if reading my mind. "Mexico. Hawaii. Iceland. I see the books you check out at the library. The maps you trace your finger down when you're in bed. I know you, Penny, and I know your heart is restless. So know this, too: I will make it happen for you one day. Somehow. Some way." He kissed me. Softly. Making me melt the way I did the night we met. "You're only twenty-four."

"Twenty-five in a week."

"I love you, Penny Stone."

"I love you more, Ledger."

The next week, he gave me a card with a gift certificate to the spa.

It's not Paris, but it's a way for you to indulge. You deserve it, Penny. I love you with all my heart.

My skin is ice cold now, and I stand in the bathtub, turning the hot water on, needing to burn, the memories so sharp — I want to feel the pain of them.

I get out of the shower, wrapping myself in a towel, sitting on the bed with hair dripping wet. Opening the laptop, I enter the password — still the same.

I know who Ledger Stone is.

There is no doubt that he loves me.

But Ledger is more than the man I know.

Before we met, he was Henry James. And I have no idea who the hell that person was.

CHAPTER 17

In the search bar, I type in Henry James, Vancouver, Washington.

My eyes run across the screen, and I click the few results I find, most of which are irrelevant — obviously different people. But there are a few links that lead me where I want to go.

The brief Internet biography adds up to what I knew about my husband and the things Emma shared. It's just, it's not Ledger's life — it's Henry's. He graduated from Rocky Point High School, attended Portland State University, and he worked for General Motors.

Frustrated at not finding more, I sit back against my pillows, staring at the photo of Ledger and me on my bedside table. The two of us, hand in hand, at Wild Deer Lake last summer. I wish I could go back to that moment, pull his face to mine and ask him, "Who are you? Who are you really?"

Would he have told me the truth?

I type in *Ledger Stone*, assuming I won't find anything besides the recent truck wreck. He isn't on social media, so there are no profiles to click through. But as I scroll past the current news stories, I find an obituary in a foster parent newsletter.

An obituary for Ledger Stone that is twenty years old. A shiver runs over me.

Pulling it up, I bite my bottom lip, wondering if this Ledger is my Ledger.

A bright-eyed boy, full of life, energy, and optimism, Ledger Stone, born November 3, 1990, passed away March 22, 2001, leaving the world better than he found it. Which is saying something for a boy who faced so many hardships and overcame so much in his eleven short years on earth.

We (George and Cecelia Mendoza) had the privilege of being Ledger's foster parents for a little over a year, and in that time, Ledger repaired our clocks, fixed broken bicycles, rewired a radio, and learned to change the oil in the Buick. A handyman who never had the chance to grow into his own, we will miss him dearly, as will his foster brother and our biological children.

The world tragically lost a wonderful boy due to a forest fire, but our hearts are more full for having known him.

Emotion pricks my eyes as I reread the brief and heart-felt words of Ledger Stone's foster parents. The name may be a coincidence, but I glance back at the words *his foster brother* and can't help but think about the fact my husband was a foster child too.

He never said much about his time in foster care. It was hard on him, becoming a ward of the state when he was eight, after a birth mom he could hardly remember relinquished her rights to care for him. He spent the rest of his childhood bouncing around foster homes. It was difficult, he said, and he didn't like thinking about the past. But when the twins were born, I remember him cradling them in his arms, eyes glistening with tears. "They will always know I love them."

That memory alone propels me to dig deeper. My husband, the father of my children, loved us. He wouldn't hurt us.

Does that mean he is really gone?

I copy and paste the date listed in the obituary and type Clemente County, the area where he went to high school. When nothing comes up right away, I add in the words *foster child*.

There's a hit.

Clicking on the new article, I draw a sharp breath. Emotion no longer pricks me, it rushes through me. Tears flow from my eyes as a new picture begins to take shape. A picture no mother, no child, should ever have to see.

> *Sunday night, a forest fire swept through Clemente County. While most people evacuated safely, two young foster boys, age eleven, were found in a home during clean-up. One child was taken to a hospital to receive immediate attention. The other boy did not survive the fire.*
>
> *The foster parents are grief-stricken, as is their close-knit community. The deceased child was in custody of the state at the time of his death and has no known relatives.*
>
> *Donations can be made to Foster Kids Kamp in his honor.*

I understand why the newspaper wouldn't include the foster boy's name, but I need to know if this Ledger Stone is the person my husband decided to become after he died. My fingers flex, both scared and desperate. As I enter the names Ledger Stone and Henry James in the search bar, I add 'foster care' and 'Clemente County'.

The top article that pops up is from 2001, a month before eleven-year-old Ledger died. My heart pounds as I click on the story, trying to make sense of the tragedy.

> *Foster Kids Kamp holds fortieth Annual Box Car Derby. The event was held to raise money for the social service program that funds summer camps for local foster children. There was a wonderful turnout, and foster children showed off their wooden cars before racing them.*
>
> *Derby winners were foster brothers Ledger Stone (first place) and Henry James (second). When asked about the*

race, Stone said, "It was awesome building the cars with my
Henry. He's so good at it."

James' response? He laughed good-naturedly, his dim-
ples a clear sign that he was having a good day. "Ledger
taught me everything I know. We may be kids racing box
cars, but one day we're gonna work on real cars together."

The event raised a record amount of money, which will
allow sixty-five foster children to attend camp this summer,
giving them the happy memories that they deserve to have.

It's hard to breathe. The picture painted by what I've
just read is so tragic, so unfair. Two little boys, alone in the
world, surrounded by flames. Imagining my husband, sitting
next to his closest friend as he took his final ash-filled breaths,
causes me to keel over. Why has he never told me this? This
event must have shaped him deeply, yet he buried this story
along with so many others.

And Henry James grew up, went to college, met and
married Emma.

And then, at some point, he "killed" himself and became
Ledger Stone. Taking on the name of this foster brother he
knew and loved. *"We were sword fighting with sticks." Ledger laughed.*
"He won."

Fresh tears fill my eyes for the story I don't understand.
What happened after he met me? And where is he now?

A knock on the bedroom door startles me, and a head
pokes through. Emma.

"Oh, God, I'm so sorry, I can go . . ."

I wipe my eyes, shutting the laptop. "It's fine." I'm
underdressed, in only a towel.

"I brought you a treat. There's a cupcake shop in town.
There were so many choices, I hope you like red velvet." She
holds up a white box.

"Oh, thanks," I say, standing and moving to the bathroom. I close the door and slip on my robe, tying it tightly
on my waist.

Emma sits on the edge of my bed. "Maybe it's a bad time but, um, I wanted to talk to you, Penny. I know there's been so much going on, but . . . we never really talked about, well, about our husband."

I nod, understanding. It's been four days since Ledger died, three days since Emma came to my doorstep, two days since I was told my husband's accident was a suicide.

It's so hard to swallow this as truth. I've been trying to ignore reality, but Emma is here, and as she hands me a cupcake, I can't hide from it anymore. She is here, trying to reconcile this, same as I am.

But she was married to a different man than I was. A man with a college degree and a well-paying job and stability. Looking at her, with her long hair so straight, her make-up so pink and pretty, her skin so flawless. Her clothes so lovely. It's hard not to be jealous.

I don't want to begrudge her the nice things she has, that's petty and immature, but it stings. And I wonder if that is what drove Ledger away. If he was used to that life and then he married me, a short step up from the trailer park. Maybe . . . maybe he resented giving up so much to be with me.

No, it can't be that. He loves the twins. So much.

"What do you want to talk about, specifically?" I ask her, setting the laptop on the bedside table.

"Do you think there's another woman?" She bites her bottom lip, still convinced that he is with wife number three.

"He loved me, Emma. He wouldn't have left—"

Her eyes lock on mine, sharp and hard. Hurt. "He loved me too, Penny."

How do I explain that the love we shared was bigger, deeper, than the love she thinks she had?

Even as I think it, I know how pathetic I sound. Who do I think I am? That my love is the purest, most true? He didn't love me enough to tell me about the fire that took his foster brother's life.

"Did you know about, uh, the fire? When he was little?" I ask, my fingers over the terrycloth edge of my bathrobe.

Emma's shoulders fall, trying to see where I'm going with this. I only want to find the truth.

"Of course," she says finally. "That fire is what made him the man he is."

CHAPTER 18

The words hang in the air. I sit, staring at the woman whose words have rocked my world, and my heartbreak over the fire turns to fury. How dare the man I married — had two children with — tell her things he never told me?

"You didn't know," she says, her words soft, comforting. "Oh, Penny. I'm sorry."

I wipe the tears from my eyes. "It's fine. I just need . . ." Pressing my fingertips to my temples, I try to think what I need.

"Details?" Emma asks.

I nod. "I'm completely in the dark here."

"I get that," she says. "And I wish I could help, but honestly, I don't know much."

I look up at Emma, so polished. I haven't seen her frazzled. Emotional, yes, but she isn't hanging on for dear life like I am. It's not fair. I'm a good wife and mother, I do my best at work, I try hard, and yet . . . my entire world is unraveling. And it feels like the woman looking back at me is holding the cards. I just want to see her hand.

"Anything is better than nothing, Emma."

She nods, her fingers running along the edge of the comforter on the bed. "I know it made him protective of people he cared about. Like, he was always so worried about something happening to me. He hated to leave me alone."

I nod, trying to reconcile that version of Ledger with the one I know. "He'd leave me for weeks on end," I say tightly. "Guess he overcame that struggle."

Emma's eyes widen. "Oh, I didn't mean anything by that. Maybe he just changed."

I nod. "Or maybe this marriage, this life, was never real to him," I say, doubting my husband in a way that sends equal waves of shame and sorrow through me.

"I wish I knew more about what happened in that foster home," Emma says. "But he hated talking about it."

"I need more than this," I say, exhaling. "I need to understand him better."

"I don't think I can help with that," Emma says. When I don't respond, she rises from the bed. "I'll give you some space."

When she leaves, I pull on clothing, twist my hair into a bun, and reach for my phone, shoving it in my back pocket. As I take the final sip of the watered-down iced latte, I know what I need to do. I need to go to the gorge. See the place my husband was before he went missing . . . before he died . . . before whatever the fuck happened.

In the laundry room, Jack has the washing machine up and running. "You fixed it?"

He grins. "What do you take me for?"

"Thank God. Our landlord takes forever to return my calls."

"You rent this house?" Emma asks.

I nod. "Yep."

She smiles, but it's crooked. "That's so great," she says finally, her words overly cheerful. Overcompensating.

Jack lifts his eyebrows. "You have a place in Vancouver?"

She nods. "Yeah, I still live in the house Henry and I bought."

It hurts, even though by now I shouldn't be surprised by a single thing she says. Of course Ledger was a homeowner. He was so many things before he knocked me up.

"So, uh, I was thinking, since Bethany has my kids for the afternoon, I'm going to take off for the rest of the day. I'll ask my mom to come over to help with the kids when they come home from the park."

"Where are you headed?" Jack asks.

"Just out. I have some errands to run." My phone rings and I answer it, ignoring Jack's question.

"Hey, Pen, I'm so sorry," Bethany says, her voice filled with frustration. "But Thomas is sick. He just threw up all over the splash pad."

"Oh, shit, do you need me to come help?" Emma and Jack perk up, listening in.

"No, it's fine. I already have all the kids in the van. I'm just so sorry. I know I offered to babysit."

"Don't even. I'm fine, I swear." When I end the call, Jack and Emma look at me expectantly.

"What's up?" Jack asks.

I explain the situation, and Emma speaks up. "I can babysit. You should go do whatever you had planned. You've had a hell of a day."

"Really?" I don't want to tell her where I'm headed. For some reason, I need to do this alone. Get the facts for myself.

"I can stay," Jack says. "At least until five."

"You're sure? I won't be back until—" I look at my watch. "—seven or so."

"It's fine. No need to call your mom, either," Emma says. "Jack and I can handle two adorable kiddos."

* * *

Thirty minutes later, I'm on the road after saying goodbye to Clementine and Benjamin. They were bummed about leaving the park, but once they saw their babysitters, they were happy.

Jack slipped me a hundred-dollar bill before I left. "What's this for?"

"Treat yourself to something. Dinner. A movie. I don't know, something to get your mind off everything."

101

I thanked him and left, not telling him that the last thing I want to do is stop thinking about Ledger. I want to think about him right now more than I ever have before. Which is saying something, considering how enamored I'd been when I met the man. Borderline obsessed. I loved Ledger so damn hard it's difficult to remember that time without cringing a little. There were no ifs, ands or buts about it. He was mine.

He was also Emma's.

I drive with the windows down, filling up my gas tank at the edge of town and grabbing a Diet Coke and a bag of Sour Patch Kids. Vance Donovan's name flashes on my phone screen. I take the call, driving toward the mountain pass with sugar in my veins and an adrenaline rush. I have no idea what I'm going to find — if anything — but I have to see this place for myself.

"Hello?" I say, my voice tight, sharp. Refusing to sound small.

"Can you come in tomorrow? I have some things I'd like to discuss."

"Can't you tell me over the phone?"

"No, actually, it's best in person. Does 1 p.m. work? Here at the office?"

"That's fine," I say, my words clipped, ending the call and turning up the volume to the radio.

It's a two-hour drive, and by the time I near mile marker 141, it's four in the afternoon. Pulling over on the shoulder of Marshadow Pass, I turn off the ignition, unbuckle, squeeze the steering wheel for strength before I open the door.

The air is hot, and a dry, forceful wind rushes over my skin. Grabbing my keys and my phone, I walk to the spot where the guardrail was busted through, a temporary one in its place. The wreckage has been cleared from the highway, of course, but as I look over the gorge, I see the remains of the semi-truck.

There are so many splits and crevasses in the gorge that it's impossible not to feel the depth of all of this. My stomach clenches and I feel ill, clutching myself in horror as I imagine the fall, the loss, the great unknown. Imagining my husband falling, falling, falling, so damn hard. Gone.

When we met, it was a crazy fall. Head over heels in love with nothing to lose. Everything to gain. Reckless kisses and making love uninhibited in a hotel room, young and wild and so damn free. A freedom I tasted for such a short sliver of time.

And all the time he had a story he didn't share.

Why?

My heart pounds as I consider this.

The shock of the answer hits me hard, and I drop my phone. It bounces off rocks, off the high gorge walls, into the river rushing below. My phone is gone. My clarity intact.

Maybe Ledger wasn't trying to hurt me.

Maybe he was trying to protect me.

But protect me from what?

CHAPTER 19

Without a phone, I drive straight home, wanting one thing and one thing only: to wrap my kids in my arms. Everything inside me feels unsettled, unsure — but they are my one true thing.

Jack's car isn't in the driveway, but Emma's is still here. I look at the clock on the dash; it's just after six.

Inside, the house is quiet — which is a surprise. The sun is still high overhead and the heat of the summer day is relentless. "Hello?" I call.

Clementine runs to greet me at the front door, wrapping her arms around my legs. "Mama," she says, burying her face in my dress. "I missed you."

Behind her, Emma follows. "Missed her? But I thought we were having so much fun together, Clem?"

The nickname isn't one we use, but I smile all the same. "Did you have a good time with Emma?"

Tiny holds out her hands. "She painted my nails pink!"

"Fancy," I say. "Where's your brother?"

"In timeout. In his room," she says, matter-of-fact. My eyebrows lift and she continues, "Emma said he was being naughty."

I look at Emma, confused. "Naughty how?"

Emma shakes her head. "Not naughty, I said he was *sleepy*."

Clementine looks up at me. "Can I finish my show, Mama?"

I nod. "I'm going to go check on your brother."

Emma tells me she's going to finish up the dishes from dinner as I head toward Benny's bedroom. The door is closed tightly and I press it open, finding my little boy curled up in a tight ball, facing the wall. The room is dark, the blackout shades drawn. Stepping toward the bed, I whisper his name. "Benny boo, it's Mama."

Crawling into the bed, I wrap my arm around him, kissing his head. His body is heavy, sweaty with sleep. His shoulders rise and fall with each breath and I close my eyes, my breath matching his.

Naughty or not, he was surely sleepy. I press my hand to his forehead, feeling a slight fever, and I wonder if he caught what Thomas has. The timing for a sick kid isn't great, but it's better that he is sleepy than my daughter's words *he was being naughty* being true.

Still, I can't shake that unsettled feeling and, standing, I head back to the living room, leaving Benny's door open a crack.

In the living room, Clementine is snuggled on the couch with Emma. It's not that I don't like the sight, but it feels slightly too personal. How much do I know about this woman?

Nothing, really.

A wave of nausea washes over me. Shit. Maybe I'm getting sick too.

The timing is all wrong, and I'm exhausted for a hundred and one reasons. Knowing I need to choose my family over Emma's feelings, I thank her for watching the kids.

"It's no problem," she says, standing from the couch. "Clem is such a doll."

"And Benny, he just seemed really tired?"

Emma nods. "Yeah, Clementine had gone inside to use the bathroom and I was in the backyard with Benny, right after Jack left. He wouldn't stop yawning, and he said he was really tired."

"And he was crying," Clementine says. "Remember? He was crying a lot."

My chest tightens. "He was upset?"

Emma nods sympathetic. "Yeah, poor kiddo. Kept saying how much he missed you. Once he was in bed, though, he calmed right down. He fell asleep in minutes."

The story slightly eases my discomfort, and I walk Emma to the door. Clementine stares at the television as the next Netflix show comes on. "Again, thank you so much."

"Were you able to get some things done?" she asks, reaching for her purse from the bench by the door.

"Yeah, but I'm drained."

She holds up a hand. "You don't need to say another word. If you need help with the kids again, I'm here."

"Don't you need to get back home? To a job, or . . .?" My words trail off. I don't even know what she does for a living. I know nothing about her. How insane am I? Just leaving my kids with her this afternoon? No, Jack was here too, for most of it. I'm not crazy. *Am I?*

"I don't work at the moment," she says. "And I was hoping to stay long enough to get some closure. It feels so unsettled still, doesn't it? Like I was saying earlier, do you have any thoughts about another woman?"

I bite my bottom lip. "All I have is what Jack told me."

"About the unknown number?" she asks.

"You know about that too?"

She squeezes my arm. "Jack and I have spent a lot of time together the last few days. And we've talked. It's been good for us both, I think."

"What do you mean, good for you?"

"Well, Jack and I both care deeply for the same person."

I stare at her blankly. "Jack cares about me, about Ledger. He's ours. Mine."

Emma lifts her eyebrows. "I'm sorry, I didn't mean . . . is there something between you and Jack? I didn't realize. I thought you and Ledger were—"

106

I shake my head. "No, that's not what I was saying. Of course not. I love Ledger. I just mean Jack's *our* friend. Not yours."

Emma twists her lips, and pity is written in her eyes. "Oh, sweetie, I never meant to hurt you. It was your idea for Jack and me to get dinner together the other night."

Frustrated, my voice rises. "I don't care about you and Jack. God, Emma, I just — look, I feel a little claustrophobic, is all."

"Understood," she says, backing away. "I never intended to overstep."

My face flushes hot, immediately ashamed for my outburst. "You didn't," I tell her. "It's just been a long day. I'm exhausted and don't feel well."

Emma has been nothing but sincere. And here I am yelling at her for helping me, for telling me her story and listening to mine. I slept with Ledger when she was still his wife. I had his children, made a life with him. She should hate me. But instead she stands here with sympathetic words, tender eyes and a soft heart. She painted Clementine's nails pink, for goodness' sake. She isn't the monster.

But then, who is?

CHAPTER 20

I give Clementine a bath, sitting on the floor next to the tub, one ear listening for Benny in case he wakes. I add lavender to the warm water, wanting to believe it will have a calming effect on her as much as on me.

"Is Papa gone forever?" she asks, dipping her plastic doll in the bubbles. "Thomas said he was never coming home."

I run my fingertips in the bubbly bath water. "Thomas doesn't know everything, sweetie."

"Do you?" She runs a plastic brush through the doll's hot-pink nylon hair.

I sigh, leaning against the wall. "I only know a few things for sure, sweetie."

"Like what?"

"Like the fact that you are my sunshine, my stars and my moon."

She beams. "The whole sky?"

I get lost in her pine-green eyes, lashes thick like the boughs of a tree. "The whole world, even."

"I thought I was your whole world," Benny says, sneaking up on us.

I pull him into my lap. "Hey, little sleepyhead. You feeling okay?"

"Yep." He scrambles from my lap, pulling off his clothes. "I want to swim, too."

I help him into the tub and watch as my two peas in a pod splash with their bath toys. "Hey, what happened?" I ask, reaching for his upper arm where a bruise is forming in a ring.

He shrugs, pushing a plastic tugboat through the water.

"No, Benny, why do you have a bruise?"

He's not listening, singing the Baby Shark song with Tiny.

Not wanting to upset either of them after the week we've had, I drop it. I sit on the bathroom floor, letting them wear themselves out. Feeling grateful that my phone is lost, deep in the gorge. Maybe Ledger is down there somewhere, lost and alone, looking for a sign.

Trying to find his way home.

There are a few things I know for sure. My love for Clementine and my love for Benjamin are two of them.

My love for Ledger is another.

Crazy, maybe. Lovesick and insane. In the deep end without a paddle.

But maybe not. Maybe I can love a man who lied to me and cheated on his wife and defied death once and maybe twice. Maybe love is more complicated than I ever thought. And maybe it's going to be okay.

Meeting Ledger Stone changed my life, my dreams, my everything.

If he's gone, truly gone, I won't ever get over that loss. He's not just any star. Since the day we met, he's been my guiding light.

I lean my head against the bathroom door as the kids shriek in delight over the game they've just invented. A smile spreads across my face as I remember being in this bathroom with Ledger a year ago. It was the end of an awful week.

The twins were being so naughty; they'd started a game that involved purposefully wetting their pants. They thought it was hilarious, but I was tired of running laundry and trying

109

to explain how this wasn't an acceptable game. My mom offered to take the kids, and I happily handed them off. Ledger was excited — a night with me, all to himself. I snort, thinking about how disastrous it went.

"Why are you laughing, Mama?" Benny asks, tugboat in mid-air.

"No reason," I say, smiling, my hand on the faucet, adding more hot water to the tub. But there is a reason. I'd been in such a sour mood that night after taking the kids to my mom's apartment. A short story of mine had been rejected from a fancy-ass literary magazine, again, and I was so angry. Jealous and bitter, and I told Ledger I didn't want to go out. I wanted to drink white wine and take a bath.

Ledger was looking forward to having fun with me — he'd just gotten back from the road. But he didn't argue. He let me have my moods — it's one of the many things I love about the man. He knew I could be a roller coaster of emotions, but he never once looked for a way off the ride. He was in it with me, holding my hand even if we were screaming for dear life.

I stripped out of my clothes, my leggings and my sweatshirt, in my bra and panties, and Ledger wasn't even trying to get any action. He knew that was off the table. His job was to get me in a bath with a glass of boxed wine and talk shit about the magazine editors while I cried.

But when he started to draw the bath, the entire faucet ripped out of the tile. Rotting drywall and years of buildup meant our bathtub was a rusty vortex that needed to be dealt with.

I was pissed. I slumped to the floor, feeling like nothing was going right. And instead of sinking to the tiles gracefully, I tripped on one of Tiny's Barbie dolls and fell over, into Ledger's arms. He caught me — of course he did. I was practically naked and he was the love of my life and I moved closer, sinking my body against his as the bathtub filled with dirty water. He kissed me hard as I cried for the stupid short story and the twins' stupid game and the stupid rental house with a broken bathtub.

110

But honestly, I knew none of it was stupid. I loved writing and I loved the twins and I loved this house because the moment we moved in, we made it a home.

"Don't give up," he told me after, kissing me on the bathroom floor. "Not on your dreams. Life's too short to quit when it gets hard."

Ledger didn't quit on me. And I can't quit on him.

He might be missing, but that doesn't mean he's gone.

* * *

When the kids are in bed — my bed — I crawl in beside them, the lights off, front door locked. I'm used to Ledger being gone for weeks at a time, to being alone in the house — but things feel different tonight. Going to the accident site changed things for me.

If Ledger didn't tell me about Emma, there must be a reason. Something I am overlooking. And I've been too distracted with the other potential reasons he is gone to consider why he left the first time.

Pulling his laptop into my lap, I enter the password and once again crawl into a rabbit hole that will have me free falling fast.

This morning, reading about the fire he survived, seems like ages ago, but the images of him and his foster brother scared and alone as a fire engulfed the home where they lived are as fresh as the sight of the river deep below the mountain's edge, the remains of the semi-truck a heap of metal in the belly of the gorge.

As I type *Emma James* into the search bar, I try to focus on the screen, not the pounding of my heart, my trembling fingers. There's a photo of her next to a Facebook profile, an Instagram feed and an alumni article from PSU.

I click on the Facebook profile first. But it's set to private and all I can see are a few photographs. All of them are of her poised and polished. Selfies at the beach, at a restaurant, in a garden.

And the last one is of her with her husband. *My husband.*

There is nothing else, though. No stories, no highlights. And when I click onto her Instagram feed, there's nothing besides the exact same handful of photographs. It makes no sense. Emma comes across as so full of life, so sweet, like the popular girl in high school with shiny hair and a bright smile. The kind of person who would be all over social media showing off her perfect life.

But what is perfection anyway? Does anyone actually have it? Tears prick my eyes, because maybe losing her husband changed all of that for her. Maybe she withdrew and lost connections. Maybe she's been grieving for five long years.

There needs to be something more I can find. A piece to the puzzle I can't quite fit.

I type in her name with the county where she lives. *Emma James, Clemente County.*

And something I'm not expecting pops up in the search results.

Her name is listed in the public records of arrest.

It won't let me click on her name, though; won't let me see what the arrest was for. Only that it took place six years ago. The top of the page reads: *If you would like more information, please contact the Office of County Records.*

Bile rises in my throat, and fear twists knots in my belly. I run to the bathroom, retching up my uncertainty. I didn't realize I could feel so sick so often like this, but I've never experienced this sort of pain before. This kind of shock. I lean against the cabinet under the sink, trying to catch my breath, exhaustion weighing down on me in a way I've never known. I close my eyes, taking deep breaths, and then, panicked, they pop wide open as I think back to when I last had my period.

Counting back days, I realize it was only a week ago — there's no way I'm pregnant. And if I'm being honest with myself, I've felt bone-tired for a lot longer than a few days. It's been months of feeling depleted. It was one of the reasons Ledger insisted we get physicals a while back. I'd pushed it off, saying I would take an iron supplement, that maybe I should cut back my shifts at the diner for the summer. But he made the appointments, citing some article he read on his phone about the mental workload women carry and how he wanted to up his game. I'd been appreciative, even if the appointment was anti-climactic. According to the nurse practitioner, I was in good health, just an overworked mom of preschoolers.

Now, though, I feel a different kind of weary. A whole new kind of tired. A tired that stretches out across my entire life. If Ledger is gone . . . and I'm supposed to solo-parent for the rest of my life . . . No, I can't go there yet. I squeeze my eyes shut, not wanting to imagine such a thing, willing myself to focus on why I felt so nauseated in the first place. Emma.

There could be a hundred reasons why the woman had been arrested. And I won't find out tonight. God, I wish I had something more concrete to run with.

What was Ledger trying to protect me from?

Before I can answer the impossible question, though, there's a knock on the door. My heart leaps from my chest. My head pounds.

Wiping my mouth on a towel, I stand, looking at my twins, bodies entwined, a box fan facing them, a white sheet over their small frames. Walking down the hall, the knock comes again, and I pause, unsure. Wishing. Praying. Wanting the person on the other side to be Ledger. An impossible hope. But my hope nonetheless. I want to ask him what the actual fuck is happening. I want to look in those dark-green eyes and pound my fists to his chest and tell him whatever he's doing is not okay.

I want him to be here. On my doorstep.

I can't imagine him leaving me.

But I can't imagine him dead, either. Jordan Parrish is wrong. This wasn't suicide.

So what was it?

There's another knock. Softer this time.

I pull open the door, drawing in a sharp breath as I do.

Is this who Ledger was protecting me from?

CHAPTER 21

Emma stands on the doorstep, suitcase in hand, looking exhausted.

"Hey," I say, uncertainty twisting my core. "What's up?"

She groans. "I'm sorry, I tried to call but you didn't answer."

"I lost my phone."

"I'm sorry, I shouldn't have come."

"What happened with the hotel?" I ask.

Emma sighs. "The plumbing at the hotel is busted. My room is flooded."

"I see." I bite my bottom lip, knowing what she wants. To stay here. But her name is listed in the public records of arrest. She could have been arrested for any number of things. And the truth is I don't want to upset her. I suddenly feel like I'm walking on eggshells. "You can sleep on the couch," I tell her. "I don't have a guest room or anything."

"You sure? I don't want to impose."

I swallow, biting back my words. If she didn't want to impose, why would she be here at all?

But I don't say that. I open the door and let her in, glancing down the hall where my two little ones sleep in my bed.

"Just let me grab some blankets and a pillow from the laundry room."

"It's awesome that Jack was able to fix the washer."

"Yeah, Jack has been a great family friend for the last few years. It seems like we've known him so much longer."

"Jack and Henry, I mean Ledger, met through work?"

I nod. "Yeah, he helped Ledger get the job as a trucker." I lean against the doorframe, trying to decide how I want to play this out with Emma. On one hand, she is clearly hiding something. On the other, if I don't press for information, who will?

"Would you like a drink?"

Emma's eyelids raise, and she reaches for her tote bag. "I brought tequila. Want to do a shot?"

I snort, assuming she's joking, but she's off the couch and in the kitchen cupboards, grabbing two small glasses. "Uh, okay. Sure?"

She pours the alcohol, and I look in the fridge for a lime. I find one and slice it. "Sorry, I need this and salt if I'm doing this."

As we toss them back, I can't help but think how odd this is. What would Ledger think of Emma being here? God, I wish I could ask him. The thought of him never returning, never being next to me, has me reaching for the tequila. I pour us another round. Then a third.

By now I'm feeling the effects of the booze — my head buzzes in a delightful way, and the sharp edges of my life begin to blur. We move back to the couch, and I sink against the cushions. "It's so strange to think of Ledger going to college, having his life so put together."

Emma lifts her eyebrows. "Not exactly put together. We never even got ourselves a life insurance policy."

"We didn't either," I say. "Strange he wouldn't have insisted we get one, considering . . ."

"Considering it made things extra hard for me after he supposedly died?"

"Yeah, I mean, without Ledger's paychecks, we're kind of screwed." I groan, not wanting to get into money with her.

"Sorry, I don't want to burden you with all that. It just seems so fucking irresponsible."

"If he was lying about who he was, maybe he was scared to get himself a policy. I mean, clearly he forged documents for himself, but maybe he was scared to go to that extreme."

"Maybe," I say, unsettled by her words. "But you don't have a job, right?"

Emma sighs. "I worked when Henry was alive. I live off my mother's estate. So I don't need to work now."

"That's good. But what do you do all day?"

She groans. "I sound pathetic, don't I?"

"Not pathetic. Sounds like it's been hard to move on since he died, is all." Saying the word *died* seems so bizarre . . . because the true words are *since he faked his death* . . . but saying that to Emma would feel callous and cold, even if it's true.

And suddenly the whole situation exhausts me. My buzz from moments ago fades fast, and now all I want to do is get in my own bed, press my nose against Ledger's pillow and breathe him in. I need to hold on to what I have left of him.

Standing, I put an end to the conversation for the night. "Give me a second to grab some blankets."

I enter the laundry room and grab what I need to make Emma a bed. As I walk back into the living room, she's setting down her purse and suitcase, slipping off her shoes. I stretch out a sheet over my second-hand couch and ask if she's hungry, if she needs something else to drink.

"No, I'm fine, Penny. The tequila is going to help me sleep, that's for sure. And I just really appreciate this, being in your home. You feel like family."

"Do you have much family near you? You mentioned your mom."

She shakes her head. "Technically, my mother is close by. But she lives in a home for early-onset Alzheimer's now."

"I'm so sorry." I spread out a quilt and fluff the pillow.

"It's life. You can't really pick the cards you're dealt, can you?"

"I don't suppose you can."

"Not to pry, but have you been crying?" she asks. "You looked a little . . . upset when you answered the door."

"It's just been a long week. And I haven't been feeling well."

"I bet it's the stress. Have you been sleeping?"

"Actually, sleep has been the one thing I haven't lost in all of this. When I sleep, it's like this whole nightmare isn't happening."

She sets a hand on my arm. "I think I'll go home tomorrow," she says. "Let you grieve without having the constant reminder in your face that Ledger was a sociopath."

I flinch at the words. "Ledger isn't crazy."

She presses her lips together, and her head tilts. She thinks I'm the one who has lost her mind. She excuses herself to change in the bathroom, and I try to collect my thoughts until she returns. This whole day feels off. The morning with the busted washer, the drive to the gorge where I saw the depths that Ledger would have fallen. The idea of him surviving that fall is impossible.

Maybe Jack is right.

Maybe it's time for me to come to terms with the possibility that my husband is really, truly dead. Brake failure or not, Ledger may never be coming home.

Emma walks back into the living room, setting her clothes in her suitcase, now wearing leggings and a tee-shirt, her hair in a not-so-messy bun. Still looking so poised. "Well, regardless, I think I'll be leaving in the morning," she says again. "I've got a lead on wife number three, and I'm going to see what I can find out."

My heart pounds. "A lead?"

Emma nods, biting her bottom lip. "I didn't want to mention it, not until I know more. But I want to keep everything out in the open with you."

I feel conflicted. The thought of her leaving before I find closure doesn't sit well with me. If this woman was arrested, I want to know why — what for — before she leaves town. But if there is really a chance Ledger is with another woman . . .

My throat goes dry, and I realize I don't want to know. The closer Emma gets to the truth, the sooner I will have to face the reality of the truth.

I'm not ready for that.

"Look, Emma, don't rush away on my account. It's still only been a handful of days, and maybe there is something we're overlooking here."

"Yeah, like wife number three. I'm telling you, Penny, you're a sweetheart, but you're being naïve. I know it's hard to accept the idea that the man you love no longer loved you," she says, pressing a fingertip to her mouth. "But we need to look into this unknown number, ask people who knew him what might have been going on. I've been poking around the last few days and—"

"You what? Who have you been talking to?"

"The guy at the gas station down the road, the bartender at the pub he went to all the time with Jack. I've been asking questions because I've waited five years for answers. I feel close to finally getting them."

"And who is this lead?"

She steps over to her purse and pulls out her phone. "It's not much, but I hacked into Ledger's Google account and found this in his calendar."

I stiffen. "You hacked his email?"

She swallows. "I had to, Penny. I need to understand what happened to the man I love. If there is a shred of hope that he is still alive, I need to look into his eyes and ask him the question that I haven't been able to shake since the moment I saw his face on the news."

"And what question is that?"

Her pale-blue eyes fill with tears. "Why wasn't I enough?"

My heart tightens on those words. "I hope you get the chance to ask," I say. "Because that would mean he is still alive."

I want to hate her, feel scared of her, kick her out of my home, but also . . . I want to understand her. This woman my husband loved in some way, at some point in time.

"What did you find in his calendar?"

"He was meeting with someone named Holly last week."

"Holly?" My brows narrow as she turns her phone to me so I can read the screen. "I don't know anyone named Holly."

Emma exhales, her face as tense as I feel. "If we want to find Ledger, we need to follow this lead."

CHAPTER 22

In the morning, Emma says she is heading back to the hotel to see if her room is available again. While she's gone, I get the kids in the car, deciding to go to Over Easy for breakfast. It's been several days since the accident, and I want to see Cheryl, but more importantly, I want to see if Sheriff Lawson is there like he usually is before his morning shift.

The diner is bustling, but Benny and Tiny are comfortable here, and they run right over to Cheryl, who scoops them up in her arms, calling over her shoulder for Johnny, the cook, to start making some silver dollar pancakes for the kids. I slide into an open booth, and Cheryl walks over with a pot of coffee. "Oh, sweetie, look at you."

I snort. "That bad?"

"I don't mean that, I mean you've had a hell of a week. I'm surprised to see you is all."

"I wanted comfort food. And to talk with Sheriff Lawson. Has he been in?"

"Not yet. But I'm sure he'll be here soon. French toast and bacon?"

I nod. "And hash browns."

"Coming right up, along with two hot cocoas, extra whipped cream."

Clementine and Benjamin smile up at her before reaching for crayons in the plastic cup on the table and drawing on the paper placemats.

Leaning back into the familiar booth, I let my shoulders fall. It's the most peaceful I've felt in days, lifting the coffee to my lips and watching my kids doodle happily. Several regulars walk over, patting my shoulder, giving me their love, winking at the kids and letting me know I'm not alone. In any of this. And it's comforting. The concern is real, the care is genuine. These people are my family as much as anyone.

When the food arrives, the kids douse their pancakes in so much syrup I can't help but laugh. Right now if they can find pleasure in a sugary sweet breakfast, I won't begrudge them that. In fact, I do the same.

With a forkful of French toast in my mouth, I see Sherriff Lawson walk in. "Just sit tight, okay?" I tell the twins and slide out of the booth as Lawson finds himself a stool. I sit next to him as Cheryl gets him his coffee. He seems surprised to see me.

"Hey there, Penny. How are you, hanging in there?"

"Been better," I say, twisting my lips. We look over at the twins, and he smiles.

"Those kids of yours are pretty sweet. Saw your mama last night, she was pretty torn up."

"Were you at the bar?"

He nods. "Yep, and man, Penny, I just can't picture Ledger doing that to himself — taking his life."

"I can't either," I say. "And I don't think he did."

Sheriff Lawson frowns. "But the reports, everything says he did, Penny. What are you suggesting?"

I swallow. "I'm not sure. But I know my husband. This isn't him." I pull a piece of folded-up paper from my back pocket. I printed the information from the website this morning. "I need to know why this woman was arrested."

"Emma James? Who is that?"

"A woman who might know something about Ledger. I found this online, but it doesn't say what she was charged with."

"Well . . ." Lawson runs a hand over his jaw. "She may not have been charged at all. People can be arrested for all sorts of things."

I nod. "Can you help me?"

Sheriff Lawson folds the paper and slips it into his shirt pocket. "Of course. Want me to call you when I get the report?"

"Actually, I lost my phone. Can you call my mom? Leave a message with her?"

"Of course."

"Thank you," I say, blinking back tears. "I just need answers. I need to move forward, and right now I can't."

"It's all right, dear," he says, patting my hand. "Losing someone you love—" He sucks in air from the side of his mouth. "—it's hard to come to terms with."

"I'm gonna go finish eating with the kids," I tell him, not wanting to argue that I believe Ledger is still alive. "Thanks so much."

"Don't mention it. Hang in there now."

I finish eating breakfast with the kids, and Cheryl tells me the meal is on the house. I ask to use her phone before I go.

"Of course, don't even think about it," she tells me.

I enter my mom's phone number and wait for it to ring, looking around the diner. So many familiar faces, all of them with sympathetic eyes. Tiny and Benny are talking with Tom, a retired vet who's hiding quarters behind his ear. They're enthralled by the magic trick.

"Mom?" I say when she answers.

"Penny, where you calling from? I've been trying to get ahold of you all morning. You've had me worried sick."

"I know, Mom, I'm sorry. I lost my phone yesterday and haven't gotten it replaced."

"All right, you doing okay?"

"Yeah, we just had breakfast at Over Easy. I'm on Cheryl's phone right now."

"Can I help you with anything today?" she asks, satisfied with my response.

"Actually, yeah. I have a meeting this afternoon with Vance Donovan."

"All right, I can come to your place or you can bring the kids here."

"I think they'd probably like the change of scenery."

I drive home, the kids talking a million miles a minute, high from their sugar-fueled breakfast. When we get inside, I help them pack their bags quickly, and as I'm sitting on Benny's bedroom floor, I feel so tired I could fall asleep.

"Maybe we should take a little nap before we go to Grandma's," I say, reaching for a fluffy blanket on Benny's bed. "Come here, guys, let's get cozy and take a nap."

"Can we watch a show?" Tiny asks. I tell her sure. She races off then comes back with a tablet, pulling up Netflix.

"Just lie here with Mama, okay?"

Tiny and Benny must realize I'm overwhelmed with exhaustion, because they put a pillow under my head and pull the blanket over my body. "I love you, Mama," Benny says, curling up next to me. I close my eyes, breathing in my two little ones, falling asleep before they've even chosen a show.

I wake to someone calling my name. I jerk up, stirring Tiny as I do. "Shhh, it's okay, sweetie," I tell her, but her eyes won't stay closed. She and her brother are both sitting up, awake. All three of us must have been sleeping hard. I check my watch, shocked to see two hours have passed.

"Penny," Mom calls again, in the house now. She pauses in Benny's doorway, seeing the three of us in a cocoon of our own making. "You scared me to death." She has a plastic bag and she hands it to me. "You can't live without a phone, you had me terrified. Burned through a pack of cigarettes when you didn't show up."

"I'm so sorry," I say, yawning as I stand, taking the bag from her. Inside is a disposable cell phone. "I didn't mean to worry you."

"I'm just glad you're okay. The thing that really scared me was Sheriff Lawson calling. He said he needed to talk to you. What's going on?"

I swallow, wondering what the verdict is. What Emma was arrested for. "Nothing, Mom," I say as the twins give my mom hugs. "I mean, nothing to worry about right now." I'm not going to get into Emma's potential criminal history in front of my kids.

"Well, what do you two say, pool day at Grandma's?"

They smile widely and I finish packing their bags. A few minutes later they're driving away in my mom's sedan, and I go inside to splash cool water on my face. Looking in the mirror, I can't help but notice how sunken my cheeks are, how dark the circles are under my eyes. Ledger going missing has aged me like nothing else. I'm twenty-five years old, too young to have wrinkles this deep.

I rip open the plastic packaging for the cell phone, knowing my mom asked me to text her my number once I set it up. But it needs to charge first before it will turn on, so I plug it in, anxious to call Sheriff Lawson.

I go back to Benny's room for the tablet so I can look up his phone number and jot it down on a scrap of paper in the kitchen. I make myself a pot of coffee and fight the perpetual yawning. Frustrated with my incessant need to sleep, I consider Emma's words from yesterday — maybe it's the stress of all of this getting to me.

Sighing, I realize that maybe I *should* see my doctor. The thing is I was just there a month ago, getting a routine physical. Ledger and I always put off stuff like that, but we have insurance now that covers annual exams.

Still, I don't like how worn out I feel — so utterly on edge — and maybe it's time I at least do something to help me with my sleep so I sleep at night instead of feeling like a zombie all day. I decide to log into my healthcare provider's site to see about an appointment. Tears in my eyes, I realize this is maybe more important than I realize. If Ledger is dead . . . if the worst has truly come to be . . . then I need to be strong and healthy for Benny and Tiny. They need me to be the best version of myself.

So I log in to the patient portal on my tablet, entering my date of birth and password. It lists the date of my last exam, the results of the screenings, and I scroll down, looking for where I can schedule an appointment.

I'm able to make an appointment two days from now, and I press confirm. Once I finish that, it auto logs me out and takes me back to the home screen. I stare at the birthdate and password log-in and bite my bottom lip.

Answers are what I need. And if Emma was brave enough to hack into his email calendar, I should be brave enough to hack into Ledger's health portal.

Taking a shaky breath, I log into my husband's account, not at all prepared for what I might see.

CHAPTER 23

It's confusing at first, the fact that there were multiple appointments made after our physicals a month ago. It doesn't add up. The fact that Ledger would have scheduled and gone to these, never once mentioning them.

My heart falls, realizing that there was an awful lot Ledger never told me. And maybe it's time to come to terms with that, like Jack suggested yesterday. My husband — dead or alive — kept me in the dark about so much. These mysterious appointments shouldn't shock me.

But they do.

There are tabs for upcoming appointments, reminders, results, inbox and medications. When I click on appointments, I see that he had another one after our physicals.

Hovering the arrow over the results tab, my heart pounds. Clicking on it, I forget to breathe.

Patient: Ledger Stone
Test panel name: Bone marrow examination
Ordered by: Dr. Holly Winters
Performed date: July 14

I reread it, trying to process the words *bone marrow examination*. Unsure of what it means, I copy and paste them into the search bar on a new screen.

Bone marrow examinations are used in the diagnosis of a number of conditions, including leukemia, multiple myeloma and lymphoma.

My vision goes blurry as I absorb that sentence, fearing the worst.

I click back to the results tab on the patient portal.

Bone marrow examination results are in.
Please call your healthcare provider to discuss.

I was hoping the actual results would be listed right here. Instead there is a vague sentence that tells me nothing.

Except that Ledger was keeping more from me than I ever imagined.

There have been so many times over the last few days I wanted to talk to Ledger, but now, I need to more than ever.

Does — did — my husband have cancer?

I set down the tablet, trying to make sense of these appointments. He went, in secret, to discuss his health. Why would he keep that from me?

Unless.

I close my eyes, the tears breaking through and streaming down my face.

Unless he was trying to protect me from something.

The time on the screen says 12:15, and I need to leave if I want to make it to the Grand Slam offices in time. I shove the newly charged phone into my purse, grabbing the note with Sheriff Lawson's number. Then I make sure the doors are locked before heading out of town.

If I had more time, I'd stop by the hotel where Emma is staying and let her know where I'll be, and my phone number. I don't owe her anything, but I feel anxious about her leaving town before I talk with Lawson. But then I realize I don't even know where she's staying.

The drive to the corporate office is quick, my mind in such a fog, trying to imagine Ledger knowing he has cancer and holding that back from me. It seems impossible.

When I arrive on the third floor, Vance is waiting for me. This time his gray face is even more ashen. And I know that whatever he has to say isn't good.

I shake his hand before he leads me to his office. And I brace myself for whatever he might say next.

"I'm sorry that it has come to this, Penny. I know you've been through quite an ordeal in the last week, and I hate to burden you with more."

"Did you show people the documentation Ledger made?" I ask, this being my one and only hope.

Vance nods. "I did." He sits down opposite me, behind his desk, and he pulls out a file. This one is thicker than the one he had last time, and I wonder just how many notes have been made about the man I loved. Love.

I don't know what is real anymore.

"Mrs. Stone, a dozen inspectors have gone over the truck, trying to piece together exactly what went wrong the night of the accident."

I nod, my throat dry. "And?"

"And we found something rather conclusive."

"Which is?"

"Some Grand Slam trucks may have been overlooked in terms of regular maintenance, and there are some well-thought-out points that Ledger has provided our teams regarding proper wear and tear on the trucks we have our drivers operate, but Ledger's truck was in top shape when it went over the guardrail." My heart falls and I close my eyes, but Vance continues. "Except for one thing," he says.

"What's that?"

"The brakes were damaged."

I sit up straight. "They were?"

He nods. "Our men worked alongside the police department, and I can assure you that they will be calling you to verify what I'm sharing now. But Penny, it's not what you want to hear."

I bite my lip. Not what I want to hear? Vance Donovan has no clue what I want to hear. I don't even know what I want to hear at this point. That Ledger's alive and a liar? That he is dying of cancer? That he is off with a third wife? That he loves me? That this was all a misunderstanding?

I don't know what would be better. Because really, what is worse? My husband is either alive and a liar, or dead and a liar.

And either way, our marriage was a joke. Not even legal. He is Henry James, not Ledger Stone, and none of this is real.

"What did they find?" I ask, my eyes now dry, my voice cracked and broken, my hands in fists. I want the fucking truth.

"The brakes on Ledger's truck had been tampered with. They had been cut halfway. Which means they were messed with intentionally, so that the vehicle would go over the guardrail at a steady pace — not fly off the cliff. It means this was no accident."

"What are you saying?"

Vance clears his throat. "Look, Penny. We have video footage of Ledger the night before his death. Your husband was alone. He was depressed and taking Benadryl, and he cut his brakes before he went over the guardrail."

I shake my head. "No, Ledger wouldn't do that."

I try to look for more words to say — more evidence to prove that my husband was stable — but right now I don't know what to think. The Ledger I fell in love with wasn't even a real person.

Which makes me wonder, how can I defend a man I didn't even know?

"Unless the police provide us with proof that someone did this to Ledger, we have to believe he did this to himself."

"That's insane," I say, rattled. "You know that, right? It literally makes no sense."

"Company policy, I'm just the middleman." Vance sucks air between his teeth and my stomach rolls. It's all feeling much too final. But I don't even know what to do to fight back. "All I know is what I've told you, ma'am. And until further notice, this case is closed."

CHAPTER 24

What's that song by John Lennon? That says life is what happens when you're busy making other plans?

Shaking, I walk out of Vance Donovan's office, stepping into the elevator. I go down to the ground floor, into the half-empty parking lot, into my dinged-up minivan, and I close the door and I scream. Loud. Loud. Louder still.

There were no other plans.

Life, the one Ledger and I shared, was lived paycheck to paycheck. We were in it, we weren't disengaged and half-hearted. We were all in. It was our one life.

Except it wasn't.

Ledger had another life before we made one together.

And now he is gone and I am alone and what does that mean?

It means everything I thought was true wasn't.

I steady my breath, trying to understand.

Why the hell would he do this? Cut his brakes and go over the edge and die?

As I am about to turn on my van, I see Jack walking out of the building I was just in. I honk my horn, getting his attention.

His eyes lift, seeing me. I roll down my window, wishing there were a cool breeze today. There's nothing but heavy, thick air around us, and when he leans against the window with his elbows, concern is written on his familiar face.

"What are you doing here?"

Jack shrugs. "Had to drop off some mileage reports." He looks me over and I wonder what he sees. He sees enough. "What happened?"

I run a hand through my unruly hair, wishing this conversation wasn't happening. "It's bad."

"How bad?"

I laugh, sharp and hard and tight like my belly, like my heart, like my memories. So tight it all just might snap.

"Hey, why don't we get some food? I bet you haven't had lunch," he says. "My truck's just over there."

Numb, I get out of my van and follow him, wanting someone else to make the decisions right now. I don't trust myself. My instincts are off.

All this time I truly thought Ledger was alive.

I climb into Jack's truck, and it smells like Ledger. Oil and grease and sweat. It's a truck that belongs to a man, fast food wrappers at my feet, Thermos of coffee on the bench beside us both. He turns on the ignition, and country music plays.

It's music that sounds like Jack, not Ledger, and I wonder if that will be my life from now on. Looking at people and finding the differences between them and the man I loved.

The man I met in a diner, whose eyes locked on mine and I knew. I knew he was mine. And I thought it was forever. Now I'm being forced to reckon with the fact that it's not. Tears fill my eyes, and I hate this. Crying for a man who killed himself. But he did. He's a thousand things I don't understand right now. His life is a question that I will never have answers to because only Ledger can answer them.

Jack can help, he can tell me it's going to be okay, and I can believe him. Emma will be here telling me she understands, and I can choose to believe her. Bethany can help me with the twins. And Cheryl can bring me a casserole. And Mom can lend me money and it will be okay. My life will be okay.

But I don't want okay. I never wanted okay. I didn't want okay before I met Ledger. I wanted the South of France. I wanted Rome. I wanted crepes in the street and coffee on cobblestone sidewalks and I wanted rooftop glasses of champagne. I wanted more. I wanted it all. And what do I have now? Nothing but empty promises and a life written in lies.

We drive to a burger shop, and Jack parks the truck, and I watch it all happen but none of it feels real. How can any of this feel real? My life was with Ledger. That was a life I understood.

Jack takes my hand, squeezing it tight, and I look at him. Tears are in his eyes too, and I know he knows.

"It's over," I tell him. "Ledger killed himself. He's dead. Grand Slam just showed me the reports."

"That's not possible," Jack tells me.

"Yes, it's true." I lift up the file. "Everything is in here. All the information you need to believe. It's really over. Ledger died. It was no accident. He did this to himself."

Jack slams the steering wheel with his fists. "Fuck," he shouts. Screams. "Fuck, fuck, fuck, fuck. No."

I understand his fury. His anger. His wrath.

"It can't be true," he says. "They missed something. What about the unknown number, the person who called him? Emma said he had some girl, some lady named Holly."

"It was a misunderstanding. Ledger was sick. I don't know how sick, but sick enough for him to be seeing a doctor. A doctor named Holly. When he got those phone calls, it must've been her. He saw her several times. She was a physician at our family practice."

I don't use the C word. Don't admit that Ledger might have had cancer, because I don't know. And what would it change? I don't want to deal with that too. I don't want to tell people that on top of everything else, Ledger created more lies, kept more secrets.

"Shit," Jack says, shaking his head. The burger shop in front of us is called Fancy Freeze. The signage is in big red block letters advertising milkshakes and French fries and hamburgers and I want them all. I want to stuff my face and eat until I'm too full and get sick. I want to numb myself.

"Can you get me lunch?" I ask Jack.

He does. He gets out of the truck and orders our food and I wait, biting my nails and staring at the brown folder in my lap. Too scared to open it. To look at the truth again. My husband is dead. I am a widow. Twenty-five years old and I am a widow. I have no money and he is gone and now what am I supposed to do?

The tears fall so hard, I can't see. It's hard to breathe, and when Jack gets back in the truck with the food, I tear open the bags and I eat. I don't speak. I hand him the folder and I eat my food and let him find out the rest on his own.

He reads the report. As I dip my fries in ketchup, as I eat my cheeseburger and drink my shake, I let him keep on reading. The reports from Grand Slam. The reports from the police officers. The photographs of the brakes. The conclusive evidence that points to one end. My husband is dead. And he killed himself.

"They had to have made a mistake," he says at last.

"You got through all that and think there was a mistake made?" I shake my head and wipe my greasy fingers on a paper napkin. "This wasn't a mistake, Jack. This was intentional. Maybe they can't prove that Ledger cut the brake line. But his fingerprints were there because it was his truck."

Of course he doesn't want to hear it. I don't want to hear it, who in the world would want to hear this? But it doesn't change anything.

"I think they must have fucked up somehow; it's a company, what do they know?" Jack asks. "What are you gonna do, Pen? If it really was intentional, you won't get . . . There won't be any money for you, Penny."

I laugh. So sharp it hurts, like it could cut me like a knife. "I don't care about the fucking insurance money, I care about Ledger. I care about the fact he died. The fact he lied. Everything I thought was true isn't. That's what I care about, Jack. Not some fucking settlement I don't deserve."

Jack runs his hand over his forehead. "It's not some fucking settlement, Penny. Maintenance errors like this, like Ledger documented, you could be looking at $5 million. A real payout. That would set you and Benjamin and Clementine up for the rest of your lives. You need to be thinking about them now, thinking about the kids."

I feel sick. "You think I don't know what I need to be thinking about? Jack, they're my children. Of course I'm thinking about them. I'm thinking about how I'm going to cover rent next week, I'm wondering how I'm going to keep the electricity on. You don't think I'm thinking about them? It's all I think about. All I've thought about for five fucking years. I'm their mother first. I was Ledger's wife second. And now he's gone, but my priorities haven't changed. I'm taking care of Tiny and I'm taking care of Benny, and I don't need Grand Slam's money for that."

"I know you don't, Penny," Jack says, taking me by the shoulders and trying to talk sense into me. "I know you can do all of this on your own. You're the most beautiful, smartest, most confident and capable woman I've ever known." His eyes are on mine, so, so tight. "I know you like to pull yourself up by your bootstraps, but maybe you don't have to. Let me help you. We can make this easier than it is right now. If you had a payout, you'd be set for life. Think about that."

"Why do you care so goddamned much whether or not I get a payout from Grand Slam? I don't want to cheat them. I don't want to lie."

"But he lied to you," Jack says, his voice gone cold. "And you took it for five years. And for what?"

"I love him," I say, my words seeming feeble and small.

"You shouldn't suffer because he took his own life."

I point to the folder, wiping my eyes. "The evidence is pretty damning. It would never be reversed."

"People can write stories with all sorts of endings," Jack says, his words an echo of Bethany's. "How's yours gonna end?"

CHAPTER 25

Jack drives me back to my minivan, both of us in silence. We are both at a loss for words. Ledger is dead.

Before I leave his truck, I thank him for the food. For caring so much about me. For wanting what's best for the kids.

"It's you I care so damn much about, Penny."

"I'm not yours to have," I say, blinking back fresh tears. Then I close the door, not sure where this conversation leaves Jack and me. I'm upset with him for his intentions, but I don't yell at him, I don't fight. I don't tell him I think attempting to reverse Grand Slam's decision is impossible. It's not my fight, getting him to believe me, see things the way I see them.

Jack is a grown man, and he can do what he wants.

But I know that I don't want to fight Grand Slam over this. Not right now. Right now, I just want my kids. I want them in my arms, in my bed, a blanket over us, creating a cocoon away from the rest of the world. Nothing else makes much sense, but they do. They are my heart and my soul.

I thought Ledger was too, but I was wrong. Our love has changed. It has taken on a new shape now, a shape I don't yet recognize. Maybe I never will.

I drive to my mom's, wiping my eyes as the tears fall, wondering just how I'm going to tell the twins that their father is gone forever. I don't want to. But there are a lot of things I don't want to do right now. Like put one foot in front of the other. Wake up and buy groceries and go to work.

I want to hibernate.

When I get to Mom's apartment, I open the door, scared to see her face. The moment she sees me, she'll know.

"Mom?" The apartment is dark, the air conditioner is on, the shades are strong. Benny is sleeping on the couch, a cartoon on with the volume low. Mom is in the kitchen, her eyes opening wide in alarm as she takes me in. My tear-stained cheeks and my red-rimmed eyes. She knows.

"Where's Tiny?" I ask.

"Oh." Mom frowns. "Emma came and got her. She said she talked to you, that it was fine?"

My stomach drops at the mention of Emma. I never called Sheriff Lawson to get the details of the arrest report, but now that I know that woman has my daughter — without my permission — my worst fears fill my head.

"I didn't tell her she could take her. I haven't seen Emma all day." My voice is high and shrill. "When did she take Tiny? Where did they go?"

"Honey." Mom is shaking her head, stepping closer. "I think they were going to get their nails done at Orchid Nails. She said it was fine, that she was gonna take Tiny home afterwards. You never called me with your new number, so I couldn't check with you, and she said she'd spoken to you at the house before you left for your appointment in Tacoma."

"No, she didn't tell me anything," I say sharply. "How long ago was this?"

Mom looks at her watch. "Maybe an hour ago?"

"Benny," I say, walking over to him and picking him up off the couch where he is sleeping. "Hey, baby, we gotta go now, okay? We're gonna go home, all right?"

Mom stares at me, confused. "Penny, calm down—"

I cut her off. "Mom, I'm not calming down, you don't understand. After the day I've had, no. Everything is out of control. I just need Tiny with me."

I grab Benny's bag, my car keys are still in my hand, and I pull open her front door.

Behind me, she shouts for me to stop. "Just calm down, Penny, talk to me for a second," she says.

But I don't listen. I'm already down her steps and sliding open the back door of the van, buckling Benny into his car seat.

"Just give me a second to catch up, tell me about the meeting," she says. But I'm in the driver's seat, pulling away, and I don't stop to listen, don't stop to talk. I need my daughter. Right now. All I need are the two loves of my life in my arms. Not with Emma. A woman I don't know, a woman that maybe I should never have trusted.

I get to the strip mall where Orchid Nails is situated, and I see Emma's shiny car. I park in front and unbuckle Benny quickly, dragging him into the salon with me.

Tiny's eyes meet mine right away, and there's a bright smile on her face. Thank God. She is here. In one piece. Alive.

Emma stands, shocked, confused. I march over to her, pointing a finger in her face.

"Don't you dare tell lies to my mother about me. About conversations we've had. I never told you that you could take my daughter. Don't you dare lie about my children again," I shout.

And maybe it's not fair. Maybe it's not justified. To take out all of my fury, all of my anger at Ledger on her. Maybe she doesn't deserve it. But she did lie to my mother. And that sends up enough red flags right now, rings alarm bells. Makes me question everything and everyone.

Tiny's polished fingers aren't yet dry, but I don't care. I can repaint them later. She's four years old and I never told Emma she could take her. Tiny cries, confused and scared, and the women at the salon are looking at me as if I am the monster. As if I am the villain. And maybe I am. Whose story is this anyway? It sure as hell was never the way mine was supposed to go.

Supposed to go. What does that even mean? I was never *supposed* to get knocked up when I was twenty years old. I was never *supposed* to fall in love with a man I just met. I was never *supposed* to marry a liar, a cheater, a fake.

I was *supposed* to live happily ever after. I was *supposed* to make my dreams come true and I was *supposed* to be strong enough to do that.

At least I can still be that. I may not be perfect, and I may not have chased many dreams. But I will chase this one until the day I die. I will fight for my children. Even if their father won't.

"Don't you dare talk to me again. And if you so much as lay a finger on my children, I will call the police."

Emma looks at me as if I'm crazed, but I'm not. I've felt unhinged plenty of times this week — but not right now. Customers getting their nails done look at me as if I'm a monster, but I'm not ashamed. I hold my head up high as I take my children from the salon, tears running down Tiny's face, confusion on Benny's; he's still probably half-asleep.

I don't know much, but I do know this: I never asked to be a mom, but here I am, a mother.

And above all else, I will protect my children until the day I die.

Turns out I'm all they've got.

CHAPTER 26

When I pull up at my house, Bethany is outside in her front yard. Thomas is running through the sprinkler, and she waves me down. I walk over to her, knowing she's been so good to me, so faithful over the last two years, and she's probably anxious with worry.

"I haven't seen you all day, everything all right?" she asks. Her baby is in a sling against her chest, and I feel a twinge of longing, wishing I could return to that time. When the twins were small enough to wrap against my body. Bethany's eyes soften as she searches mine.

"I wouldn't say I'm all right. It's been pretty rough. And I just . . ." I close my eyes, pressing my fingertips to my temples. "I'm so tired and so scared."

"It's okay," she says, patting my back to comfort me. Oddly enough, it works. "What can I do?"

"Honestly, right now, just knowing that you're next door is enough. I need to be alone tonight, but I want to know I'm not all alone, if that makes sense?" Benny and Tiny have climbed out of the car seats and are running over to Thomas.

"It makes perfect sense. You're in the house all by yourself." She kisses her daughter's head. "I saw Emma in the driveway earlier."

I frown. "Really? If you see her again, will you text me?"

"Of course, but is your phone working? You didn't reply to my texts all day — not that you need to, I know you have a lot on your plate."

I groan, reaching into my purse for the phone my mom bought me this morning. "I lost mine yesterday. I got this cheap burner phone until I can replace it. Here. Let me text you right now with the number."

As I try to enter Bethany's phone number, my fingers feel like fudge, sticky and thick, and I can't concentrate. Everything from the day is piling up and making me dizzy.

I drop the phone, and as I bend down to pick it up, my knees give out. I fall to the pavement, tears in my eyes. "Dammit." The phone screen is cracked, but so is my heart. "I need Ledger to catch my fall, Bethany, but he isn't here. I'm alone. I'm all alone."

Bethany is at my side, and it's her hands that reach out and take mine, that stroke my hair and hold me close. "Oh, Penny," she murmurs. "This is all too much."

"Emma took Tiny from my mom's today. She totally lied to my mother too. And to think she was here, looking for my kids. Snooping around." I wipe my dripping nose with the back of my hand. "It's weird, right?"

"It's weird," Bethany confirms. "I don't trust her, Pen."

"I know, but like, I can't trust anything my husband said either. He was lying about more than his past, Bethany. He was lying about his future."

"What do you mean?" she asks, both of us sitting on the ground cross-legged, the kids running in circles, occupied with a game of tag.

"He had cancer."

Bethany gasps, covering her mouth with her hand. "Oh, God, Pen."

"I know. And I think . . . I think he knew that if he died, I'd be left with nothing. I think he was hoping I'd get a settlement from Grand Slam."

"You think he did this on purpose?"

I press my fingertips to my lips, choosing to trust Bethany with information that could destroy my family all over again. "I don't know what to think. But we don't have life insurance. Something like cancer treatments and being out of work . . . it would have ruined us financially."

"He really had cancer?"

I explain to her what I saw online. "I'm going to the doctor's office tomorrow. I need answers. Right now, everything just feels out of control."

"Emma being around doesn't help anything."

I nod. "I know. I don't want her around the kids anymore, I made that crystal clear."

Bethany squeezes my hand. "Pen, if Ledger really did this . . . to himself . . . for you . . . what does that make you feel?"

I wipe my eyes and look up to the bright blue sky. My voice breaks but my heart stops racing. Stops pounding like the beat of a drum. It slows for a moment as I consider the gravity of his love for me. "If he chose to die so that we didn't have to pay for his treatment, it makes me so angry. Because I would have wanted the chance to talk him out of this. But," I shake my head, biting my bottom lip, "it also means that he wanted to take care of me and the twins. It means he chose us, in the end."

The tears fall harder now, and I let Bethany hold me until the sobs stop wracking my body, until I can steady my breath, until I can manage to pick myself up off the ground and stand.

"Want me to get your kids fed and in bed tonight?"

I shake my head. "No. I want to be here for them right now, it's really all I want."

She nods in understanding. "Call me after the doctor appointment, okay?"

"Kids, come on," I holler. "I'll warm us up some food." There are plenty of choices from the offerings friends have dropped by over the last few days.

They whine, wanting to stay and play with Thomas, but I don't give in. Knowing the look in my eyes, the sound of my voice, they run over without being asked twice.

They know me.

Ledger is gone. He won't look in my eyes and he won't hear my voice and he won't know what I mean without me having to say a thing. Because he is dead. Gone. I am alone. And I feel so, so lonely.

"I love you, Pen," Bethany says. I look over my shoulder, my eyes on my dear friend, grateful to have someone in my corner who is so good to me. She hasn't had it easy. She's fought for the life she has, and as I push my key into the lock, opening my door, I know that I'll fight for my life too.

* * *

Inside, the house is buzzing; the fans have been on all day, and it shows. For the first time in a week, there's a breeze pushing through the screened windows, and I close my eyes, dropping my purse, my keys, stepping out of my shoes. The kids trail me as I pull open the refrigerator.

"Mama," Benny asks. "What's wrong?"

Ignoring him, Tiny splays out her hands. "My nails are all messy." She grumbles, annoyed, and I understand. I'd be annoyed too. I *am* annoyed too.

More than annoyed — angry.

"I'm just tired," I tell them. "And I miss your papa. I miss him so much. I want him home."

Tiny and Benny start crying, both of them scared. And I'm scared too. They may be small and I may be grown, but it doesn't make a difference. Right now, our fear is the same.

"I miss him, too." Tiny's voice cracks. Tears fall down her face, and I wipe them away and kiss her cheeks. I pull Benny close. "I miss him so much."

Maybe he's watching over us right now. I don't know. It's hard to believe in God when you see your father beat your mother when you're a little girl. It teaches you a few things about God. About how real he is, about what angels looking out for you really means.

Because when I was little, I never felt guardian angels spreading their wings, offering me protection. I didn't believe in God when I was small, and I don't believe in God now.

But that was before Ledger was dead. Before I was looking at my children, trying to think how in the world I am supposed to tell them that their papa is never coming back. It was before I ever had to take their small hands into my own and find words to explain what happened.

Maybe I never really needed God before. Or maybe I just never knew what sort of God I needed. The God I need now is one who would understand that life is really fucked up and really unfair. A God who understands forgiveness in ways I don't. A God who understands love in ways I can't.

I want to. I want to forgive and understand. I want to love Ledger in spite of his flaws. Despite the secrets. Despite his past. I want to, but I can't. Not right now. Not today.

"I'm hungry," Benny says. And I nod, kissing their foreheads, patting their backs. I pull out a casserole dish from the open fridge, cheesy enchiladas, and I slide them into the microwave. I find the sour cream and two cans of 7-Up, and when I give the drinks to the children, their eyes widen in surprise.

"Really?" Tiny asks. I tell her yes, drink the soda pop. Let this sugary syrup slide down your throats. It will taste as good as the pancakes did this morning. Enough sweetness to wipe away the sorrow.

Maybe God is maple syrup. Maybe God is carbonated lime juice. Maybe God is sugar cubes and ice cream and red velvet cake. Maybe religion doesn't have to be about prophets, saviors or saints. Maybe, to some people, their salvation can lie in the everyday. Maybe God is the something sweet we need when everything else in life looks and tastes and feels like dirt.

I watch my children as they eat their dinner, and I eat mine too, feeling nauseous and numb at the same time. I look

144

around the house, the pictures of my children, my husband, our lives, hanging on the walls. And I can't shake the feeling that he's here. That he's still not gone. I know it's crazy. To think after all this that there is still a hope, a chance.

I bow my head for the first time in my adult life. I pray that Ledger is alive. Please. Please. Please let him be alive.

I look up at my children and see they're confused at what I was doing. My hands clasped, eyes closed. They don't understand. But as I look at them, I do. I understand all of it.

I know why Ledger killed himself. The shock of it causes me to gasp, drop my fork.

"What, Mama?" Tiny asks. "What's wrong?"

Grand Slam was right. Ledger's death was no accident. It was on purpose.

But it wasn't because he was depressed. It wasn't because he was running away from a life with Tiny and Benny and me. Emma was wrong about that. Maybe he ran away from her, but he would never have run away from us.

No, he had two folders on his laptop's home screen. Meticulous and organized, and that wasn't Ledger. He wasn't that neat, that tidy.

He labeled the file folder on his computer 'TRUCK MAINTENANCE INFORMATION TO BE GIVEN TO GRAND SLAM'.

No one names a file folder something that specific. That obvious. He needed me to see it. He needed me to print it out and hand it to Vance Donovan. He needed Grand Slam to believe it was an accident. That his death was caused by their negligence.

Because Ledger had cancer. And he didn't want to die, leaving me with nothing.

Ledger cut those brakes thinking it was the perfect crime. He drove himself over the guardrail.

And he died.

But it wasn't in vain.

He did it for Clementine, Benjamin, and me . . . so that after he was gone, we could live.

CHAPTER 27

After the kids are fed, given baths, and put in bed, I take a long shower, letting it run until it goes cold. When I step out, I want to wrap myself in comfort clothes, and with the towel around me, I rummage through the closet, looking for my favorite flannel: his. The red-and-white one. I grab it off the top shelf and pull it to my nose, breathing Ledger in. As I do, something falls from the shelf, and before I even put the shirt on, I bend down, grabbing what fell.

Wedged between a pair of boots, I get hold of a CD case. I smile, knowing it's something Ledger would buy — I have long given up trying to move him over to an online music account. He insists that having a physical copy of something that you can hold in your hand is worth more than the convenience of a million songs at your fingertips.

I flip the CD case over, swallowing hard when I see what it is: *Blue Hawaii* by Elvis Presley. Our song is number five, "Can't Help Falling In Love." My eyes blur with tears, the warmth of his body against mine in the parking lot of Over Easy, our hips swaying, hearts pressed together, the rush of the first night we met flooding every inch of me. I sink to the floor, opening the case, running my finger over the album art, hot tears splashing against the CD.

I hold the flannel shirt against my face, catching my tears as a reel of memories plays in my mind. Ledger undressing me in the motel, his hands covering my skin, our bodies entwined as fast as our hearts, and he can't be gone. Those memories are too few, there aren't enough to last a lifetime. I need more. I need him.

My hands shake, though, as I consider the CD I hold in my hand. Why didn't he give it to me? Why was it buried up there? I want to believe he was waiting for the right moment. That it was going to be a moment that was all ours — no one else's. Not another wife's, another woman he fell for just like he fell for me.

No. It's not possible because Ledger and I didn't fall into anything. We dove, headfirst. We swam until we were out of breath and then we went back for more. Our love was not like his and Emma's — whatever their love might have been. Ours was big enough to last forever.

So why did he have to go and leave without so much as saying goodbye? Why didn't he give me this CD and slow dance with me under the moonlight? Why didn't he tell me again and again and again that he loved me, that he'd hold on until his dying breath?

I put on the shirt and find a pair of sweats, wishing I could talk to him. I look for the phone my mom bought me, and I type in his number. It doesn't even ring — long dead. Voicemail picks up right away, and I fall into my bed, pulling the comforter over my head and burying myself in his voice.

"Hey, it's Ledger here. Sorry I missed your call. I'm probably busy watching The Bachelor *with Penny or rolling around on the floor with the twins. Catch ya soon!"*

I press redial again and again, wondering why he wouldn't have told me he was sick. If it was all for money, then he was a fool. Because money means nothing if the person you love isn't here to share it with.

I know he wanted to take care of us, but this isn't the way to do it. It's too much to carry alone, this burden of what he has done.

What he did before.

God, I hate that he married Emma, that they had a life together, a family. I don't want to share any of my memories with another woman — especially *that* woman. Someone I don't trust. If she hurt Benny . . . I press redial.

"I'm so mad at you right now, Ledger. How could you do this to me? I gave you everything. My dreams, my hopes — I forfeited all of it for you. A man I didn't even know." My chest heaves as a sob rattles through me. "Goddammit, Ledger, I believed in us. In you. And now—"

There's a knock on the front door that pulls me from my rant. And I get out of the bed, not wanting a doorbell to wake the twins. I look through the window next to the door and see that it's my mom. My shoulders fall with relief. I knew she'd show up eventually. I left her apartment so upset earlier tonight that I'm sure she's been worried sick.

I pull open the door, taking a hard look at her, feeling like shit for scaring her. She's clearly been crying and immediately pulls me into a hug, sending a current of shame through me. One second is all it takes for me to revert back to my childhood, when I wanted her approval more than anything else. I still do. I want her to be proud of me, want her to see me as a good mother, a good daughter. But what must she see right now? A twenty-five-year-old cliché of a woman who gave up everything for a man who spent an entire marriage telling lies.

But she isn't looking at me with angry eyes. No. She loves me the way I love the twins — with every fiber of my being, with all that I am and all that I hope to be. She's done everything in her power to be there for me, through thick and thin. And here she is now, on my doorstep, after dark, holding my hand. I'm lucky to have her: a woman who would do anything to make sure I'm okay.

"I'm sorry," I tell her, immediately wishing there were stronger words I could use. Embarrassment washes over me as I consider how worried she must have been after I left her house.

148

"I didn't want to come over right away. I knew you needed time to cool down, to breathe, but you could have at least called to tell me you were okay," she says, her voice cracking. "God, Penny, what was I to think?"

"You're right, but I was scared, Mom. Emma lied to you, and I think she's been lying to me."

Her brows furrow. "About what? Being married to Ledger?"

I shake my head. "No, that story all adds up. But she's too insistent on being close to Tiny. And I think she might have hurt Benny. He didn't have a bruise before I left her with them for a few hours yesterday."

"What? Why would you do that, Penny? She's a stranger. What were you thinking?"

I start crying again, my shoulders shaking. "I'm not thinking straight, that's the problem, Mom. My life is falling apart. Things have gotten really bad, really fast, and I don't really know what I'm supposed to do."

"What are you saying, Pen?" she asks.

"Ledger's dead, Mom. He's really gone." Saying the words aloud is my final straw. Tears fall down my face, and she pulls me in close, her arms wrapping around me.

"Shh, it's gonna be okay, Penny."

"Jack's been telling me to accept the fact that my husband's gone, but I wasn't ready to until now."

Bethany crosses my front yard, holding a tray in her hand. "Hope I'm not intruding too much," she says, giving me a hug. "I don't know how to fix any of this for you, Pen, but brownies make everything better."

"Thank you," I say, wiping my eyes. "Leo is okay with you being here?"

"He doesn't own me." She rolls her eyes. "But did you get an update?" she asks.

"I did," I say, leading them into the house. "But I think this conversation calls for whiskey."

In the kitchen, I pull out a bottle of whiskey, pouring us each a glass. I'm all out of white wine, but it's fine. Tonight,

I need something stronger than boxed pinot grigio. Bethany and Mom sit at the kitchen table, and I join them, shoving aside coloring books and a basket of broken crayons. Bethany and Mom watch me, anxious, unsure of what I might say next.

"I got a report back from Grand Slam." I take a sip of the whiskey, the liquid burning my throat. "The brakes were cut. And there are fingerprints all over the undercarriage. His fingerprints, Mom."

Mom covers her mouth, my words shocking her. "Why would he do that?"

It's easier to imagine Ledger accidentally going over the guardrail. It may be even easier to imagine him leaving me for another woman. But the idea of my husband killing himself? It's too much for anyone.

"He was sick, Mom."

"What do you mean he was sick?" she asks. "Like depressed? We know that."

"No, not that kind of sick. It was serious. Before I went and saw Vance Donovan today, I made myself a doctor's appointment on the clinic's patient health portal."

"What do you need a doctor for?" Bethany asks.

"I've been so stressed out and so exhausted." I see the worry on their faces and I shake my head. "No, honestly, it's nothing to worry about. I know it's because of the kids, because Ledger is gone . . . It's just so much weight on my shoulders. I made the appointment thinking that if Ledger is truly gone — missing, whatever — I can't risk not being my best self. The kids are going to need me to be strong. So I made the appointment." At this, Mom and Bethany nod, tracking with me.

"That's good, honey," Mom says. "You have to take care of yourself."

"I know," I say, swallowing hard. Because the next part is the part that feels impossible to say. "So while I was online I decided to log into Ledger's health account too. His patient portal? I was thinking maybe it would be a clue."

"And did you find something?" Bethany asks.

I nod, picking up the whiskey and taking a sip. The amber liquid burns my throat, and I stare into my glass, scared to look in her eyes. "He was sick."

"What kind of sick?" Mom asks.

"Cancer." My shoulders shake and I drop my face into my hands. "At least, that's what it seems like. The unknown phone call Jack mentioned and Emma's assumption about some lady named Holly, it was his doctor. And he had a bone marrow extraction." I shake my head, pinching the bridge of my nose. "You only have that when they think you have blood cancer or bone cancer, something really bad. He got those results and the next thing you know, he goes over the guardrail."

"Why wouldn't he tell you?" Bethany asks, her voice quiet.

"I don't know if I should talk about it," I say. "But I think he wanted me to get a settlement from Grand Slam. I think he was trying to . . ." I can't finish the sentence.

Mom seems to understand. She rests her hand over mine. "You think he did this to set you and the kids up? By blaming Grand Slam for the accident?" Her words trail off too. The three of us realize the weight of what Ledger has done.

A choice that is criminal and irreversible.

"Grand Slam isn't at fault, but Jack thinks I need to make sure that they pay."

"Why does Jack have anything to do with this?" Bethany asks.

I remember her walking in on Jack and me, the hug we shared the other day, the look in her eyes.

"There's nothing going on with Jack and me, there never has been, but he does care about me and the twins. He thinks Grand Slam will pay up and that I need to fight for that settlement money the way Ledger seems to have intended."

"How do you feel about that?" Mom asks.

I narrow my eyes, feeling more jaded than I ever have in my life. "About what? About my husband having cancer, or that he spent five years lying about his past, or about the fact that he's dead?" My voice is harsh, just like my husband's death.

"About all of it," Mom says. "How do you feel about all of it?"

"How do you think I feel? I love Ledger."

Mom gives Bethany a look. A look I know. She never thought Ledger was good enough for me.

"I know you always had issues with him, thinking I threw my life away for a man. You thought I was too young and too naïve, but I wasn't. I fell in love with a man who loved me back, and now he's gone and it's as simple as that."

"Oh, honey, it's not so simple."

"What's the alternative, Mom? Grow bitter over the fact he killed himself, be angry that he's gone and never told me goodbye? If I start down that road, I don't think I'll ever come back. I think I'll get lost in that pain. And I don't want to have my heart broken. Tiny and Benny need me to be strong. I can't lose myself in this. Ledger wouldn't have wanted me to."

Mom finishes her whiskey, angry now. "It would have been really nice for him to tell you the truth himself, wouldn't it?"

"He was trying to protect me. He didn't want me to know about the brakes, about his part in it. Probably thought I wouldn't keep my mouth shut, that I would tell Grand Slam the truth."

"And will you?" Bethany asks. "Will you fight for a settlement you don't deserve or will you let it go?"

"What would you do if you were me?" I ask her. "What would either of you do?"

Mom runs a finger over the rim of her empty whiskey glass. "I'd get the money. He screwed you over enough that you shouldn't have to pay for it the rest of your life."

"Even if I don't deserve it?"

Bethany gives me a half smile. "What does *deserve it* mean, anyways? Grand Slam has insurance against this sort of thing. You're not putting anybody out of a job, you're providing for the twins, for yourself. Ledger screwed you over. You don't need to get screwed twice."

"Did he screw me over, though?" I shake my head. "It seems like everyone is dead set on making Ledger the villain here. What if he isn't? What if he's not the bad guy?"

"Okay, play that out," Mom says. "Maybe he's not, but he did lie. About Emma, about his past. Why would you believe in him now?"

"Because I love him," I say, my voice hushed and small. Pathetic. I love a man who lied and left.

Maybe I'm the villain in the story because I let a man walk all over me until the day he died.

CHAPTER 28

I fall asleep in bed with the twins curled up against me. The clock reads 6 a.m., too early to face the day. I slept hard again, waking up with drool on the pillow, sweaty and out of sorts. It must have been the whiskey. And my body is sore from sleeping in weird angles with two four-year-olds scrunched up against me.

Still, I wouldn't trade these aches and pains for anything in the world. My children are my everything. My eyes fill with tears at the thought. I've been awake thirty seconds and already I'm falling apart. How am I supposed to pick myself up and be what the kids need when what I really need is Ledger to crawl into this bed and hold us all?

"Mama," Clementine says, rolling on her side to face me. "I miss Papa."

I kiss her forehead, her sweaty curls pasted to her forehead. "Me too, baby. Me too."

Benny wraps his arms around my waist, his cheek against my back.

I close my eyes, willing myself back to sleep. It's early, and the day ahead of us is bleak — never mind that the sun is already shining. Right now I don't care about blue skies. Right now all of our days seem gray.

A call wakes me, and I reach for the phone Mom bought me. "Hello? Mrs. Stone?"

"Yes, this is me." I sit up in bed, seeing that it's after eight in the morning. "Who's this?"

"Hello, it's Margene from Dr. Winters' office. I was calling about an appointment you made via your patient portal."

"Right," I say grabbing my bathrobe, my feet on the laminate floor. "It's for next week, right?"

"Actually, Dr. Winters requested you come in today. At your earliest convenience. It's important."

"Why?"

"I'm not at liberty to discuss this over the phone. But Dr. Winters can—"

Wanting to ask Dr. Winters about Ledger, I agree right away. "When should I come in?"

"Does ten a.m. work?"

"I'll be there."

* * *

By the time I have the twins fed and dressed and in the car, it's 9:30. Mom offers to come here to watch the twins, but they were begging to go swimming again. They've become water babies this summer, and I didn't want to take this away from them. Not when I'm hours away from learning the truth about their father.

That he's gone. Never coming back.

"Why are you crying, Mama?" Tiny asks from her booster seat.

Blinking back another onslaught of tears, I smile at her through the rearview mirror. "Mama's fine. Want to listen to the *Frozen* soundtrack?" I press play on the CD player, and they both start to sing along.

Mom is waiting for us in the parking lot, finishing a cigarette and talking to a guy on the maintenance crew. I get out of the minivan, holding the twins' hands, a tote bag stuffed with towels and suits slung over my shoulder.

"Let me help you," she says, worry in her voice, taking the bag from me, slipping Benny's hand into hers. "Let's go to my office first," she says. "It's not quite warm enough for the pool. You can draw on the whiteboard."

They happily run toward the apartment complex's office, with us trailing them. "What's this appointment about?"

"I told you I scheduled it," I say, not adding that it was bumped up to this morning for some urgent reason.

"Will you ask the doctor about Ledger, about his can—"

I cut her off. "The kids have no idea yet, Mom. I'm not ready to go there, so please don't say any more."

"They need to know their father is gone," she says in a whisper. "We need to plan—"

"Weren't you at my kitchen table last night?" I shake my head. She and Bethany stayed with me for hours, debating my choices. They both think I should fight Grand Slam for a payout, but I'm still not sure what they should be paying for.

"Jack can help you," Bethany had said. "You know he will do anything for you."

Mom unlocks the office and tells the twins to have at it. They grab a pad of Post-it notes and highlighters. After kissing my kids goodbye, I give Mom a hug. "I'll keep you posted, okay?"

Mom nods, then follows me outside to the entrance. "Please call. You keep worrying me."

I know I've put her through hell so many times over the years, and when I was younger, she did the same to me. How many men did she go through after my father left her? Enough for me to see it as a pattern and follow in her footsteps. Ledger changed all that. For both of us. He entered my life and gave me the twins and I stopped being a doormat, and she did too. We had the twins to fight for.

She's been here for me through thick and thin. And now that Ledger is gone, I will need her more than ever. "I'm sorry I worried you when I didn't call."

"Don't apologize." Mom twists her lips. "Hell, sweetheart, after the week you've had, you just need that doctor to hook you up with some meds that will erase all this."

"I don't think there is a drug for that."

She pats my cheek. "I love you, Penny, so damn much. I know I wasn't the most supportive mother when it came to Ledger, but—" Tears fall down her cheek. "—but he loved you. So much. And I hate that he's gone, for you and for the kids. I just wish I could take all the pain away."

"I wish you could too, Mom."

"You'll tell the kids soon?" she asks. "Because people are going to start talking, Pen."

"I can't have anyone knowing about the cancer. At least not until things are squared away with Grand Slam."

"So you are going to see if a lawyer can help fight this?"

"I'm not sure. But I'll decide by the end of the day. We all need to move on, one way or another."

"And Emma, have you spoken to her?"

I scoff. "After I went ballistic at her yesterday at the nail salon, I don't think I'll ever hear from her again."

"Maybe that's for the best. Just put it all behind you."

"Do you think that is what happened? That Ledger did this for us?"

Mom presses her lips together, tilting her head. "I like thinking that."

"Even if it isn't true."

"We all choose to tell ourselves the story we want to hear." She takes a tissue from her pocket, wiping her eyes. "For so long, I told myself I didn't deserve a man who cherished me. Respected me. It was easier to accept that I didn't deserve real love than admit that I couldn't find it."

"What changed?"

She nods back at the twins, who are drawing shapes on the whiteboard now. "The twins were my second shot at a love story. I messed up with you, Penny. When you gave birth to them, you gave me the redemption story I was looking for."

157

"Oh, Mom," I say, pulling her into a hug. "You didn't mess up with me."

Mom cups my face with her hands. "Penny, I did. But I got a second chance."

Tears flood my eyes as I think of Ledger.

Was a life with me and the twins the second chance he was looking for? Or did he die before he found his salvation?

I leave my mother, knowing that I won't leave the office until Dr. Holly Winters tells me what I need to hear. The truth.

I'm clinging to the fact that Ledger had cancer. I'm choosing to will it into being because that ending is so much better than any other scenario.

As I drive to the doctor's office, it's not lost on me that the idea of my husband dying this way is so much better than any other. I park the minivan, wondering if I'm the first woman to ever wish her husband had cancer.

Because if he didn't, it means he cut his brakes and took his life for one reason and one reason alone: he wanted to die.

CHAPTER 29

When I step into the office, a receptionist welcomes me. As I check in, my only thought is, what was Ledger thinking when he walked into this office alone? Why didn't he call me, ask me to come with him? I would have, of course.

Sitting in the waiting room, I can't help but be reminded of when I was waiting for the twins to come. They came early, and I delivered them, one after the other, in the hospital next to this office. Ledger was so nervous, a mess. More than that, he was terrified.

For all of us.

"Why are you so scared?" I remember asking him. I was the one with two fully formed humans inside of me, ready to enter the world. I was the one in a hospital bed with my feet in stirrups, ready to bear down.

"I just don't want anything to happen to any of you. You're my whole world." He kissed me, pushing back my wild hair, sweat dripping on my forehead.

Of course, at the time, I didn't know that Ledger had been through all this before. Rushing a wife to a hospital to deliver his child. A little girl. His daughter.

Never knew he had buried that little girl. That she was a memory, no longer a living, breathing thing. We didn't know

159

if we were having boy or girl twins — I insisted on the surprise. "Most of the surprises life gives us aren't good ones," I told him. "I'm going to take the happy ones where I can find them."

It was a boy and a girl, and Ledger let me name them both. "You did all the work," he told me as I looked the babies over, my body so weak and exhausted but my heart surging with newfound strength. My babies needed me to fight for them. I promised myself I would never, ever let them down.

It was a ridiculous promise, of course. I'm human. Selfish and self-indulgent, and I've had to say sorry plenty of times. And I was young. So young. I still am in lots of ways — but I was especially young then. I was just learning how to take care of myself, let alone these two babies.

But I didn't know how to be a wife, either, and I learned. The learning curve was steep, but the wonder in all the newness life was offering me was worth the scare of the rollercoaster.

I learned to love the ride.

Clementine and Benjamin were two pieces of my heart, and Ledger, with his raw and precious love, held us in his hands. And then, when he couldn't get up from the couch for weeks, then months — I was forced to find my own strength. And I did. I found out who I was when he was sick. Turns out I was stronger than I ever knew.

And now I sit here, in this waiting room, knowing that for this next part — this part where Ledger isn't by my side — I will be strong too.

I didn't go through so much shit for nothing. It made me who I am.

"Penny Stone?" A nurse calls my name and I stand, following her down the hall for a weight-and-blood-pressure check. After showing me into a room, she tells me, "Just change into this gown. Dr. Winters will be right in."

Alone in the room, I change quickly, noticing bruises on my upper leg as I do. I frown, not remembering how I got them.

I tie the back of the gown and sit down, waiting for the doctor. I tell myself that I won't leave until she tells me the truth about why she was seeing Ledger.

A knock on the door startles me, memories filling my mind of when Emma first knocked on my door, leading me down a rabbit hole with no answers.

"Penny?" Dr. Winters walks in. Her black hair is cropped, and her crisp white lab coat is a sharp contrast to her dark skin. She shakes my hand warmly, putting me at ease with her smile. "I'm so glad you could come in this morning."

"Of course. It sounded urgent."

Dr. Winters sits down on a stool opposite me, a tablet in her hand. "It is. In fact, it is shockingly urgent."

My eyes narrow. "Is this about Ledger? About my husband?"

She exhales, frowning, pained at whatever she needs to say next. "Yes, it is, actually. And this is such an unprecedented situation."

"Because he is dead?"

Dr. Winters nods slowly. "Yes."

"Just tell me what this is about."

She tilts her head, considering my words. "Normally I wouldn't discuss this without the patient's permission, but this situation is out of the ordinary," she says. "And you are listed as his authorized contact."

"Did you diagnose him with cancer?"

Dr. Winters presses her lips together, shaking her head. "No, Ledger didn't have cancer."

"He didn't?" I ask, the words sending a chill over me.

"No, Penny, he didn't. He had a bone marrow extraction confirming that. The extraction came back negative."

"Negative?" I stifle a sob, covering my mouth as a noise I don't recognize as my own escapes me.

I was so certain. Last night I wept over his sacrificial choice. Taking his life so we could get insurance money — knowing he was going to die anyway.

Was that the story I told myself because it was less horrific than the truth?

Tears fill my eyes as it hits me. Ledger committed suicide, just like the Grand Slam investigator determined.

"Why am I here? Why didn't you just tell me this over the phone?" I ask, wiping the tears from my cheeks.

Dr. Winters squares her shoulders, looking me directly in the eyes. "There was an error with the original blood test results both you and Ledger took. The results on file for Ledger told us his level of white bloods cells were abnormally high, high enough for me to believe he might've had blood cancer. Because of this, he had the extraction. But they were not actually Ledger's results."

I try to process her words. "So he got someone else's results?"

Dr. Winters nods slowly, as if choosing her words with care. "Yes, Penny, he did. They were your results."

CHAPTER 30

Come in this morning. It's urgent. I got that message because I'm the one with abnormally high white blood cells.

High enough to suggest bone cancer. High enough to require a bone marrow extraction.

"Give me the test, the extraction." Staring Dr. Winters down, I won't take no for an answer. "Now."

Dr. Winters is already trying to ease me back onto the exam table. I'm standing, ready to go. Wherever this extraction takes place, I need it done.

"I understand your concern," she says. "But I also am aware of the level of stress you are under at the moment with Ledger—"

"No, I need it now. Where do I go? The hospital? What? I need to know, Dr. Winters. My children . . . I'm all they have. Ledger killed himself and I . . . I'm their mother. If I'm sick, I need to . . ." I fall apart then, hard, sobbing into my hands, on the table, keeled over and broken. Alone. I want my husband here with me now. "Why didn't he tell me he was having the procedure? Why would he keep this from me? Why would he kill himself? I thought he loved me."

I'm hysterical, I realize that, but I don't care. Dr. Winters presses a hand to my arm, an attempt to soothe me, but it

163

doesn't work. I want Ledger here with me now or no one at all. I need him here. With me. I need my husband to be alive.

Why would he kill himself?

It takes time, but eventually I calm down; my shoulders stop shaking and my breath shallows and all that is left are silent tears streaming down my cheeks. Ledger is gone and I am here. And I need to know what happens next. What will happen to me next?

"The procedure can be done right here, Penny," the doctor says finally. "We will need to call someone to be with you after the aspiration and biopsy, but it won't take long, only ten minutes, and then we can run the lab results. Usually it takes a few days, but this is a special circumstance. I am hoping the lab can get us results run within twenty-four hours. I understand the urgency you feel. Well, not understand, but empathize," she clarifies. "I can only imagine."

"Thank you," I say curling up into a ball on the table. "Thank you."

"Who would you like here?"

"My friend, Bethany, can come," I tell her. "I can call her."

"After she arrives, a nurse will come in to prepare you for the IV sedation. I think this is best. Often we just have local anesthetics, but . . ." She squeezes my arm. "Let's make this as comfortable as possible."

"Would this explain my exhaustion?" I ask. "I sleep hard every night and sleep during the day. I'm constantly tired."

"Was this before Ledger's accident?" she asks, noting my comments on her tablet.

I nod. "Probably, yeah, for a month or so. And I get nauseated a lot. It's hard to keep food down. And I have weird bruises on my leg."

"This is good to know. Information like this will help us when we get the results from the extraction. But let's not jump to any conclusions. There is no need to worry ourselves until we know what the lab report says."

"Maybe that's why Ledger didn't tell me. Maybe he didn't want to worry me."

Dr. Winters' eyes soften at this. "He was very worried about you, Penny, about what cancer would mean for you and the kids. He was so scared of letting you down."

I twist my lips. "So scared of letting us down he killed himself."

"Is that what the police are saying?" she asks gently.

I nod. "Yeah, they think he did this."

"It's hard to believe that, though, isn't it?" she says.

"Why do you say that?" I ask, desperate to know Ledger's secrets, the things he kept from me. But also realizing this doctor is the first person who isn't demonizing Ledger.

"Because he loved you fiercely, Penny. You know that. Everyone in this town knows that."

"He kept a lot from me," I say. *Emma. Their child. The fire.*

"Sometimes we keep secrets for a reason."

"You think there can be good enough reasons to keep secrets that would change everything?"

"I know Ledger saw a therapist. Have you spoken with them?"

"I haven't. Do you think they would tell me something?"

Dr. Winters taps her tablet. "Let me look into that for you." She bites her bottom lip. "It's not protocol, but I can make a call."

"I'd appreciate it," I say. "I just want to understand the man I loved."

She hands me my purse, and after she leaves to prepare for the procedure, I call Bethany. My words are jumbled and messy, but somehow she gets enough information to tell me she will be here as quickly as possible.

The nurse comes into the room, and I look in her eyes, and I know. She knows. My husband is dead and I might be sick. Very sick.

It's not pity I see.

It's heartbreak.

This is not how my story was supposed to end.

* * *

As I lie on my back after the aspiration and biopsy, Dr. Winters applies pressure to the site where the syringe drew the liquid portion of the blood marrow.

"Oh, Penny," Bethany sighs, smoothing my unruly hair. She got here before the procedure began. Her eyes fill with tears as she squeezes my hand. "You're being so brave."

"I don't have a choice."

"I can have these results within twenty-four hours," Dr. Winters says. "If you need anything from me before then, do not hesitate to call me on my personal line. Okay?"

I nod numbly. "And if you hear from his therapist . . . will you let me know?"

Dr. Winters smiles softly. "Actually, he's right outside. He works upstairs and offered to come down and speak with you."

"Now?" I ask, gratitude washing over me. "Is this legal?"

"Does it matter?" Bethany asks.

Dr. Winters places a thin blanket over me, telling me that this little conversation is going to be kept just between us. "He wanted to come by and say hello, that's all."

Bethany follows Dr. Winters out of the room. I exhale, wanting so badly to speed up time to tomorrow. I need to know my fate.

"Mrs. Stone?" A man with a gray beard and wire-rimmed glasses enters the exam room. "I'm Dr. Kennedy."

"Good to finally meet you," I say, moving to shake his hand. "Ledger's spoken so highly of you over the last few years."

"I've enjoyed all the time I spent with him. It's not fair to play favorites, but Ledger was mine, hands down. He was a salt-of-the-earth man if there ever was one." Dr. Kennedy sits down, resting his elbows on his knees, clear eyes blinking back tears. He loved Ledger, that much is clear.

Dr. Kennedy is a tall, thin man in a tweed coat. He has a pencil in his breast pocket and socks with an argyle pattern. An old man that Ledger will never become. My chest tightens at this thought. And then it squeezes tighter still as I consider the fact I may never know that age either. I could be dying of cancer as I lie here.

"I understand you just had a biopsy?" he asks.

I nod. "Ledger had the same one. Did he ever talk to you about it?"

"I spoke with the police department this morning. Everyone in town has been so worried about your husband, so shocked over the accident. As I'm sure you have been."

"It doesn't feel real."

"That is a very typical response to such devastating news. If you want to see someone, to help as you begin to process this, I hope you'll make an appointment."

"I was hoping you'd help me. Now. I need to understand why Ledger would do this . . . Until this appointment, I was sure he knew he had cancer and wanted to spare us . . ." I don't say I thought my husband was trying to defraud his employer. "But the idea that he'd kill himself . . ."

Dr. Kennedy sighs deeply, devastation etched in his face. "The situation seems to point to that, but as I spoke with Sheriff Lawson, I had another thought. One you might not . . . might not be prepared to hear."

"What's that?" I ask. "Because there is nothing at this point you could tell me that will shock me."

Dr. Kennedy runs a hand over his beard. "After spending quite a lot of hours with your husband, in a client-patient relationship, he opened up with me about things he hasn't shared with anyone else."

"I know more now than I ever did before he died."

Ours eyes lock, and we hold a silent conversation. I know Ledger told Kennedy things he never told me. And part of me hates my husband for that. For keeping buried the things I wish I'd known. But the other part — the part that fell in love with Ledger Stone the very first night we met — is grateful for this doctor. For a safe person my husband could grapple through his past with. For a wise man to listen and offer support. The father he never had.

Finally, the doctor speaks. "Maybe it wasn't suicide."

"Then what? The brakes magically cut themselves?"

"No, but maybe it wasn't Ledger who did it. Maybe it was someone else," he says carefully. "Someone from his *past*."

I don't linger on the fact that this therapist knows more about Ledger's life than I do, that he is piecing this together in ways I haven't yet. I need to see Sheriff Lawson.

I sit up from the bed. "Someone like Emma."

CHAPTER 31

Bethany drives me to the police station in her van. "You sure you don't just want to go home?" she asks. "Penny, maybe you should stop and eat something. You've had a hell of a day."

"I can't stop now," I tell her, pulling out my phone and texting my mom.

> ME: *Something came up. I'll be a few more hours.*
> MOM: *Of course. The twins are going to rest and watch a movie. Later, we'll go to the park. Just text whenever you're ready. No rush.*
> ME: *Love you*

I almost type more . . . tell her that Ledger was never sick, tell her about my biopsy — but I realize I don't want to worry her.

The same way Ledger didn't want to worry me. Maybe Dr. Winters is right. Maybe sometimes we keep secrets for a reason.

"I can't believe there was a record for Emma's arrest out there and you never told me," Bethany says as she pulls into a parking space.

"There's nothing to tell until we see the report."

* * *

Bethany and I walk into the station, the powerful air conditioning sending a chill over me. "You okay?" she asks as I pause, pressing my hand to a wall.

"I'm okay, just a little weak is all. Maybe you were right, maybe we should have stopped for lunch."

"After this we'll get food. We can go to the diner."

"Don't you need to get the kids?"

"My mother-in-law came over. They're fine." Bethany unabashedly squeezes her breasts. "I'm a little full, but I can go another few hours before I'll have milk rings on my tee-shirt."

"God, I love you," I say, grateful for her friendship. Tears prick my eyes as I consider losing her, losing everyone. I can't be sick.

"Don't cry yet. Save it for the happy tears you'll have when you get the negative lab results."

I nod, pulling back my shoulders. There isn't time right now to get weepy. I'm here to see a police report, not fall apart over my children being orphans.

Stepping up to the front desk, I ask for Sheriff Lawson.

"Sorry, ma'am, he's out on a call," a young man tells me. My heart falls, and he must see it on my face. "Want me to tell him who stopped by?"

"It's Penny Stone," I say, writing my phone number down for him. "It's very important. You know what? Actually, I can just call him."

"No need," a voice booms behind me. I turn and see Lawson walking toward me. He opens his arms and gives me a big hug. I sink into it, not at all expecting that I would be so emotional in front of him but realizing that he has been around for so long, a part of my life. He has seen firsthand the ups and downs that Mom and I have been through.

"Sorry," I say, wiping my eyes as I step back.

"Don't apologize, Pen." He looks down at me in a way that feels comforting. "Come on back to the office. We need to talk." Bethany and I follow him, and he closes the door behind us. "She your backup?" He clears his throat. "Sorry,

170

that's not exactly sensitive, is it? Shit, I know you've had a hell of a week."

"This is Bethany, my neighbor and best friend. She knows everything."

"So I'm guessing you're here for the arrest report?" Lawson asks. I nod and he adds, "How exactly do you know Emma?"

"I don't know her well, but she seems to have been friends with Ledger," I tell him, not wanting to implicate Ledger in something more sinister. Such as faking his own death. Not until I have the facts on this woman.

"Well, she's a bit of a character," Lawson says, frowning as he opens a folder.

"Character how?"

"She was arrested on three accounts. Was court ordered twice—"

"What was she arrested for?" I ask, cutting him off.

"It is all domestic disputes that turned violent. She was court ordered to anger management on two occasions, and apparently she was at fault on them both."

His words hit home, and relief mixed with rage swells up inside me. "*She* was ordered to anger management. That means she was the abuser?"

"Yes, it appears that is the case," Lawson says.

I let a woman with a history of violence into my home, allowed her around my children. Bile rises up in my throat, and I drop my head into my hands, wondering how much more I can take.

"Oh, Penny," Bethany says, rubbing my back. "It's okay, knowledge is power, right?"

The words may be trite, but she's right. Information is the only way I'll ever get to the bottom of this.

Swallowing, I try to remember what truly matters here. "What are the dates, when did these incidents take place?"

Lawson looks through his file at the papers before handing them to me. "Six years ago. The other party was a Henry James, her husband, apparently. The reports were pretty rough. Over the course of three years, he had broken ribs, a skull fracture, stitches across his face. All at the hand of Emma James."

Bethany's eyes meet mine. "Holy shit," she says.

"She has a record of instability, from what I can tell — beyond her history of assault. She's not exactly safe. She was hospitalized on several accounts. How do you know her?"

"A friend of a friend," I say, still wanting to protect Ledger. From what? He's dead.

Still, it's his integrity I'm trying to keep intact because I want the twins to think their father was a decent man. Is that wrong? Is that just another way I'm rewriting our story so the ending isn't so sad?

"Well, if I were you, I'd stay away," Lawson warns. "She's trouble. You have enough going on right now, Penny."

"Thanks for looking into this." I press my lips together, debating my words. Finally, I open my mouth. "Can I ask you one more thing? Totally different topic?"

"Anything, Penny."

"If someone faked their death, how easy would it be to get away with?"

He frowns. "Who are we talking about?"

I tease my lip between my teeth. Shake my head.

Lawson must sense I'm not going to name names.

"Look, Penny, there's no reason to believe Ledger faked anything, if that's who we're talking about."

I shake my head. I'm not talking about Ledger. I'm talking about Henry James. But I can't say that.

"But it's not so hard, to be honest," Lawson says. "People disappear all the time."

"And how often are they found?"

"Depends on how good they are at hiding."

CHAPTER 32

The lunch rush is gone, it's mid-afternoon and Over Easy is practically empty. When Bethany and I walk in, Cheryl wraps me in a big hug. "How you hanging in there, sweetie?"

"Not great," I tell her honestly. "It's been a brutal day."

"Have you told the twins?" she asks as the three of us sit down on red vinyl seats in the back booth.

I shake my head. "No, I'm not ready to break their hearts." We decide on some food, and Tanya, a recent hire, takes our order. Cheryl stays seated with Bethany and me, and I'm grateful for two familiar faces, two friends whom I know I'll be able to count on for whatever comes next. Which could be anything. My entire life is up in the air.

"I saw Emma in here earlier," Cheryl says. "She cornered Jack at the counter. Was badgering him about Ledger, about who else he might have been friends with."

"And what was Jack's reaction?" I ask.

"Jack was upset. Trying to eat a burger and fries, looking at his phone. Finally he had enough and told her to back off. That she needed to leave town, stop dredging up the past. He said it wasn't good for you or the twins."

"That's good of him," I say. "I should call him. I haven't spoken to him since I got the final report from Grand Slam. I was pretty upset that day."

"Maybe wait until after you hear from Dr. Winters," Bethany says.

"What's that about?" Cheryl asks.

I wait until Tanya brings us our food — grilled cheese and tomato soup — before I tell Cheryl about my potentially life-altering appointment this morning. The bone marrow extraction.

"So Ledger didn't have cancer," she says, catching up to speed, her voice breaking. She runs her fingers over her gold cross necklace. "Oh, Penny, when will you know?"

"Tomorrow," I say, my vision blurring as I think of waiting another day until I know my fate.

"It's going to be fine. You can face anything, Penny." Bethany's words are meant to comfort me, but my chest aches, my limbs heavy, exhausted at the idea of fighting. "You aren't alone."

"I'm just so tired," I say. "So over this. My life . . . it's too much. I can't do this without Ledger. And if Emma . . ." My shoulders shake as I try to speak. "If she did something to Ledger, I will kill her."

"Emma? You think she's a killer?" Cheryl asks, her eyes widening.

"I know enough to know she's dangerous." I tell her what Lawson said. "It finally is beginning to make sense. Ledger faked his death because she was a fucking crazy person."

"Oh my God," Cheryl says. "And to think she was just here, acting like this heartbroken widow."

"She plays the part well," I say. "She came to my doorstep acting like the victim, and all the time it was Ledger running for his life. Maybe he thought she was going to kill him."

"Or kill you."

Bethany nods, leaning in. "Yeah, he faked his death a few days after you told him about the pregnancy. Maybe he thought if Emma found out, she'd go batshit."

"Maybe it was never about keeping things from you," Cheryl says, her eyes filling with tears. "Maybe it was about protecting you."

"That's what I hoped. When I went to the site of the accident a few days ago, I was standing there, looking down that gorge, thinking that Ledger would only kill himself if he was trying to protect me. But I was thinking about the wrong death. He was protecting me five years ago when Henry James died. Not this one. Because this one wasn't fake. It was intentional."

"She killed Ledger," Bethany says, her voice hushed. "We have to tell Lawson."

"I didn't want to involve the police because I didn't want them to know Ledger used to be Henry . . . but it doesn't matter anymore. What matters now is that Emma doesn't hurt anyone else."

"Why would he lie about his name?" Cheryl asks.

I think of the article, of the fire that killed his foster brother. How he lived and the other boy died. "Maybe he was already thinking of starting over."

"Remember when you two met?" Cheryl asks, blinking back tears. "You were beaming the next morning, and I knew you'd slept with him. I thought, this is trouble, because I knew what falling head over heels looked like. I'd done it myself a few times." She reaches across the table for my hand. "But I knew this was different."

"Different how?" Bethany asks.

"This wasn't any old love, what Penny felt for Ledger on day one."

"What was it?" she asks.

"This was once-in-a-lifetime love. The kind you move mountains for."

I think of the mountain where Ledger's truck went over the guardrail, his body being flung from the truck that provided us our livelihood. That truck was our saving grace when we needed a lucky break. My shoulders quake, my heartbreak a real, living thing. Ledger is gone. The love of my goddamn life.

My phone rings and I startle, lost in my wave of emotion. "Hello?"

"This is Holly Winters," the doctor says. "We put a rush on the lab work, and they were able to get me the results much faster than I anticipated. Can you come in?"

"Just tell me," I say, my heart pounding. "I need to know."

"Oh, Penny, I don't want to do this over the phone. Are you with someone?" she asks.

I look around the diner. It's empty. I set the phone on the table, putting on the speaker. "Yes, I'm with my two closest friends," I tell her.

Bethany and Cheryl reach for my hands and they don't let go. Tears fill all our eyes and I fear the absolute worst.

And then Dr. Winters confirms it.

"I'm so sorry, Penny, but the extraction tells us that you have acute lymphocytic leukemia."

I gasp. Cover my mouth. Squeeze my eyes shut.

"What does that mean?" Bethany asks.

"Acute means that the leukemia may progress quickly," Dr. Winters explains. My ears are ringing and the room spins and all I want is Ledger's arms to wrap around me and tell me I'm not in this alone. That we can fight this together. But he isn't here.

Dr. Winters is still speaking. "If untreated, leukemia this advanced could prove fatal within a few months. Which is why you need to come in as soon as possible."

"Of course," Cheryl says. "She can come in now." I hear Cheryl and my doctor exchange information, but I zone out as they end the call.

There is nothing more to hear, nothing more to say.

I have cancer.

And somehow I'm supposed to face this without the love of my life by my side.

CHAPTER 33

Bethany drives me back to the doctor's office. "You sure you'll be all right on your own?" she asks as we pull up next to my van.

"I want to do this alone," I tell her. "Then I'll go to my mom's. I'll probably just stay at her place tonight."

Bethany gives me a final hug. "All right, be brave. You are going to find out the plan of how you're going to fight this," she says, determination in her cracking voice. The words may sound tired, but right now, they're all we have. I can't just fall apart because Ledger isn't here — even though that is exactly what my heart is screaming at me to do.

Clementine and Benjamin need me. They need me to be strong. Resilient. Here.

"Thanks, Bethany," I say, pushing open her passenger door. "Love you."

"Call me if you need anything."

"You're leaking," I say, the milk rings on her top telling me she should have gone home hours ago. "You are so good to me."

Tears run down her cheeks, and she wipes them away as Tom Petty's "Won't Back Down" comes through her radio. "You have to call Sheriff Lawson."

I nod. "The moment this appointment is over, I will. But right now I just need to focus on how I'm going to fight. Ledger is gone. Dealing with Emma right now won't change that. Right now, I need to figure out how to be strong for the people who are still alive. My children."

* * *

Dr. Winters meets me in the waiting room, pulling me into a hug as if we are close friends. Maybe this is how all doctors deal with patients when they've just been diagnosed with cancer. Or maybe this is just how doctors deal with patients who became both a widow and a statistic in the same week.

She takes me into her office, walking past the exam rooms. "I know this is all unorthodox, but I don't want to wait on this."

We sit, her behind her heavy oak desk, me in an armchair. "That makes me think this is really bad."

She sets her shoulders, pain etched on every part of her face. "It is."

My body shakes, her words simple and plain and devastating. "How bad?"

"It's not good, Penny. Your leukemia is acute and very advanced."

"Would a month have made a difference? If the lab hadn't made this error?"

Dr. Winters nods, clasping her hands together and setting them on her desk. "Possibly. And honestly, I would advise getting a lawyer to work on your behalf with the company who botched the lab results. They made a crucial error that not only resulted in your husband undergoing an unnecessary procedure, but also caused you to go without treatment over the course of the last month. A month that could add or subtract months from your life."

"Months?" My throat goes dry. "I have months to live? Not years, not decades, not . . ."

"It is very advanced, Penny. It depends on how you respond to chemo, and there are some clinical trial options we can look into."

I didn't expect to fall apart now. Like this. Here, in her office, but I do. The pain of this news is so overwhelming that I can hardly see straight. My heart hurts so much I can't breathe.

The dreams I had for myself, for my life, seem so far away. Impossible. I am a widow battling cancer, the single mother of two four-year-olds who rely on me for everything.

How will I work if I'm in treatment? How will I pay my bills without Ledger's paychecks keeping us afloat, let alone pay for his memorial?

For mine.

We never got life insurance and it turns out we needed a dual plan. Because by the end of the year, our children could be orphans.

"Penny, the important thing right now is to stay optimistic. To remain in control. The timing of this is devastating, I know, but we can fight this."

It's hard to see through my tears. She hands me a tissue and I wipe my eyes. I want to be a fighter, but I feel so weak.

"Do you think this cancer will kill me?" I ask through my tears.

The heavy lines between Dr. Winters' eyes tell me she has spent a lifetime focusing, concentrating, deep in thought. She furrows them now. "I don't know, Penny. We are going to do more tests and start chemo and hope for the best. Believe that the best is possible."

"Is that what you tell everyone?" I ask.

She shakes her head, tears filling her brown eyes. "No, Penny, it's not. This isn't good. It won't be easy. And even after all of that, the statistics aren't on our side. I'm not saying this to be negative, I'm saying it to be realistic. Right now, you have so much on your shoulders, you're bearing so much. And sugarcoating this won't help you. I knew it was bad when I saw the initial blood work, and when I thought they were Ledger's results, I had him come in immediately for the extraction."

"Thank you for being honest with me," I say, bracing myself for a future so utterly unknown.

"I know you are dealing with your husband's death — but it's never too soon to start talking with a mental health-care professional. Battling cancer is one of life's most difficult fights."

"I'll do whatever I can to stay strong," I tell her. "Seeing a therapist saved Ledger's life. Maybe it can help me too."

"And there is plenty I can help with too," she tells me. "It might feel like you're in this alone, but you're not. But before we can start remission induction therapy, which is the first phase of treatment, we need to see if the cancer has spread."

"What is remission induction therapy?" I ask.

"We'd start with chemotherapy. The goal is to kill the leukemia cells in the blood and bone marrow. This puts the leukemia into remission."

We set appointments for tomorrow, for an MRI and lumbar puncture to see whether the cancer has spread to the brain or spinal cord.

I leave the office weary and exhausted — desperate to see Tiny and Benny. I need to kiss their heads and hold them close. In my van, I buckle my seatbelt, desperate to get to my mom's apartment. To tell her everything that happened today.

But before I even turn on the ignition, my mom is calling me. "Hello?" I try to keep my voice steady, not wanting her to know I've been crying for about three hours straight. Not until I can talk to her face-to-face.

"Penny?" Mom sounds rattled. "Honey, where are you?"

"In my car, I'm about ten minutes from your complex. What's wrong?"

"I'm in my car too, but it's Emma who's the problem. She tried . . . oh, Penny. She tried to take Tiny."

CHAPTER 34

"Something is wrong with that woman, Penny. You were right. And to think I let her watch Tiny a few days ago. You had a right to be mad. She seemed unhinged. Her eyes wild and, oh God, if something had happened to Tiny . . ."

My heart races, remembering the things Lawson told me about Emma earlier today. "Nothing happened to Tiny. It's okay. But Emma can't be trusted. She's more dangerous than you know, Mom."

"She tried to get Clementine to leave with her, by the swings. I saw it happening and so I grabbed Tiny. Yelled at Emma to leave us alone. I got the kids in the car, but she's following me now."

"Emma is?"

Mom's crying. "Yeah, she's a few cars behind us."

"Okay, I need you to drive to my house, okay? I need to be with the kids."

"All right," she says, her voice cracking. "I'm on my way."

"Mama?" Benny's voice breaks through the call.

I squeeze my eyes shut. Tears spilling from them. I gasp, trying to stifle my sobs. His voice reminding me what I have to fight for. "Yes, baby?"

"I miss you."

"I miss you too, I'll see you soon, okay? Really soon."

"Love you, Mama," Tiny says.

"Love you more," I say, turning on the ignition. "Okay. I'm gonna hang up, but I'll see you soon, okay?"

As I drive, I try to think of a plan. I don't know Emma's intentions, but I have to believe they aren't pure. Aren't innocent. My anger at her helps me formulate an idea of how to get her off the trail of my kids and instead, closer to me. I don't want her anywhere near my children. But I also need to have a real, honest chat with her. Namely, I need to call her out for what she did to Ledger. Not just all those years ago, but for coming to my home and playing the part of the victim when really she's the killer.

When I'm a block from my house, I turn down a side alley and park the van. As I jog to my house, I call Jack.

"Penny." He sounds both surprised and happy to hear from me. "You okay?"

"No," I say, my words rushed. "It's all falling apart. I need you."

"I'm always here for you. I need to talk to you anyways. I think I figured out how to get Grand Slam to settle with you."

"Okay, but not now. I need you to come here, to my house, in half an hour. Can you do that?"

"Are you running?"

"Yes," I say, reaching my house, out of breath. I unlock the door and step inside the house I shared with Ledger, the only place I ever really called home as an adult.

"What's going on?"

"I need you, Jack, please, I can explain later."

"Need me how?"

"Come here, please. Emma's on her way and she's dangerous. She tried to kidnap Tiny. I think she killed Ledger, Jack. I'm gonna call the cops."

"I'll call 911. You just hang tight. Do you have the twins?"

I hear knocking on the front door. "Penny?" My mom's here.

"I gotta go. My mom's here and I've got to get out. Just hurry."

"Okay, I'll call the cops and I'll be right there. And Penny, be careful," he warns. "Emma's a loose cannon."

"I know. I'll be smart. Thank you," I say, running to the door and letting my mom and the kids in.

I close it behind them, lock it. Then I kneel, pulling my children into my arms. I'm sick. A cancer is running through me, in my blood, and I don't know how long I will be able to do this. How long I will be able to pull my babies into my arms and kiss their cheeks and breathe them in. Ledger never got the chance to do this, to hold them tight before he died, and sobs escape me as I close my eyes, refusing to let them go. God, I love them so damn much and I will do anything in this world to keep them safe.

"She's gonna be here any second, Penny," Mom says. I look up into her eyes, and I see the fear written in them.

"It's okay," I say, standing, pressing my car keys into her hand. "You're gonna go out the back door with the kids. My van's down the alley. Go home, please. Jack called 911. He's on his way over. Okay?"

Mom's lips purse together. She's scared, but she has been through hell in her lifetime. She can do this.

"Mom, you're a fighter," I tell her.

"What's happening, Mama?" Benny asks. I kneel, holding his little face in my hand. I kiss him, then do the same to my little girl.

"It's okay, you're gonna go back to Grandma's and watch a movie. She's gonna order pizza and you'll have to be good kiddos until I get there."

Tiny's chin quivers, a tear falls down her face. I hear a car pull into the driveway. "You have to go, sweetheart. Be brave. Okay?"

I give them one last kiss, then tell them to take Grandma's hands and be quiet as mice. "Just walk down the alley. Don't make a sound, okay?"

My children do as I say and I lock the back door after them. They clutch my mother's hands as they walk through the yard to the open back gate, leading them down the alley.

My heart pounds as I watch them go, wondering if I am going to die, if my mother's hands are the ones they will always hold. She might very well be the one raising them, watching them grow. She told me they were her second chance in life, and maybe it was more true than we ever realized. Maybe she is going to get the chance to be more than their grandma. Maybe they will grow up thinking of her as their mother.

Tears splash down my face. The idea of losing them, of leaving this world, tears at my soul. It's not the story I want. Not the ending I'm fighting for.

But I don't get a chance to decide. Bethany's and Jack's words gave me hope, but they are just that. Wishful thinking. I hear someone knocking on my front door. Looking through the curtained window, I see Emma's car parked behind my mom's.

Without hesitation, I run to the bedroom, pulling open the safe where Ledger keeps the gun.

We can't always write the endings we want to the stories of our lives. Ledger had no choice in how his ended. Emma took that from him.

And now it's my turn to take it from her.

CHAPTER 35

I reach for the gun, hands shaking, hating that I'm even considering this. But the cops aren't here, and neither is Jack, and I'm not going down without a fight. Not now. Not when so much is at stake. How dare she try to take Tiny.

Running to the kitchen, I stash the slim silver gun in the junk drawer, not wanting to open the front door with it in my hand. Seeing the duct tape from a week ago when I hemmed Tiny's second-hand jeans, I'm reminded that I am not stupid. I'm resourceful. And I can handle this. No way in hell am I letting Emma go after my children.

Taking a deep breath, I walk as calmly as possible to the door, opening it and finding an anxious Emma on my steps.

"What's wrong?" I ask, trying to remain neutral. I need Jack and Sheriff Lawson here now.

"Hey," she says, her eyes skittering around. "I just, uh, I didn't know you were home. Saw your mom's car."

"I parked in the garage," I lie, trying to keep my voice steady. "But what are you doing here, Emma? I made it very clear at the nail salon that I didn't want to see you again."

"I know," she says, eyes glassy and tearful. "But I needed to apologize. I messed up and, um, I needed to say how sorry I am."

I lift an eyebrow. "So sorry you tried to kidnap Tiny at the park today?"

She draws back, shoulders still. "I didn't do that. I think your mom must have been confused."

"Confused like she was the day when you took Tiny to get her nails done?" Anger rises up in me. "And what did you to Benny? Because I saw the bruise."

"He was being whiny," she says, shaking her head. "I gave him a sleeping aid to get him to stop making a fuss."

I want to hit her, make her suffer — the thought running through my mind makes me recoil. I've never been a violent person. But then again, I've never had someone threaten my children.

"You medicated my son?"

Emma is visibly rattled by my words; her control starts to slip as she stalks closer to me. Her eyes are wild and red. "I crushed up a sleeping pill, but he's a brat, Penny. And poor Tiny will suffer. I'm trying to be your friend here. No one else is going to tell you the truth."

I laugh, sharp and so damn tight I'm seconds from snapping. "And then when he upset you, you grabbed him so hard you gave him a bruise? The same way you gave Henry James bruises? And a black eye? A broken rib? Just like you smashed a bottle across his face? Just like—"

She pushes me then, into the house, hard. I gasp, falling to the floor. Her strength is shocking to me but not surprising. Something about her has always been off. A bit unhinged. Desperate.

And as I look up at her, I see myself in her eyes. A mother desperate, a wife scared.

But we are not the same.

She slams the door shut, towering over me. My side aches from the bone marrow extraction and I grit my teeth, refusing to acknowledge the pain. I gave birth, naturally, to twins; I can deal with Emma fucking James.

"You think I'm stupid?" she asks, her perfect blonde bob and her perfectly pressed clothes so damn deceptive. "You

186

didn't park in the garage. I looked in the garage windows before I knocked on your door. You should have more street smarts considering how white trash you are."

"Don't do this," I say.

"Do what? Take your daughter? And why shouldn't I?"

"Because you need help, Emma. Professional help."

"Your daughter can fix this. Give her to me and I will leave you alone. I will never hurt you or speak to you. You'll still have Benny."

I sit up, my back against the wall. "You think I'll make a trade with you? Are you insane?"

She pulls a gun from her designer purse, pointing it at me. She's spun back into control now. Her hands aren't shaking. She is swinging wildly from sympathetic to psychotic, and I can't keep up. Now I'm sure, as she grips her gun, this was her plan all along. I clench my jaw, wishing I hadn't stashed mine in the drawer.

"Why should you get two of his children? Let me have one. I lost one before, and this will fix it. It will make it fair. We didn't get the man, but at least we can have his children."

"*My* children," I say, pressing my palms against the floor, willing myself to stand. "They are my children."

"It's not fair. For you to have it all." She runs to the kitchen, pointing at the photos on the wall. Pulling down the one of the four of us — Ledger, Clementine, Benjamin and me — at the ocean. So happy it hurts. Sunshine and salty air and smiles so bright and beautiful my chest aches. She slams the framed photo to the floor, the glass shattering at our feet. "You think you're so damn perfect," she says, her words warping the truth. "With the perfect life. The perfect story. The perfect everything."

"You think I have it all?" I ask, pulling my shoulders back and refusing to back down. Not here. Not now. Not ever. "My husband is dead. Because of you."

"Me?" She shakes her head, incredulous. "He killed himself one way or another."

"No. You tampered with his brakes."

"No," she shouts. "I. Didn't." Tears pour down her face. "He killed himself five years ago and he did it again last week. That's what happened."

"No," I say louder, pulling open the junk drawer where Ledger's gun is. "You ruined the brakes. You did this. It's your fault he's gone." We both see the gun.

Before I can wrap my fingers around the cold metal, we hear the front door open and then Jack is here, catching Emma off guard.

Jack. Solid and sure and always here when I need him.

Without pause, Jack reaches for her and pulls her back to his chest. Her gun is raised and he peels it from her hand. I exhale, my body trembling. I thought she was going to shoot me. Kill me.

But she didn't. I'm alive. I'm here.

"Who the hell do you think you are?" Jack asks, pushing Emma against the refrigerator, the gun to her neck.

"Don't kill her," I say, shocked at his violence. "Jack, don't do something you'll regret."

He turns to me, his eyes on mine. "Regret? The only thing I regret is not doing this a week ago. I should have killed her the moment I realized how fucking batshit this woman was."

"It's okay," I say. "Let the police arrest her. Let her pay the price for killing Ledger."

"I never killed him!" she screams. "He's off with another woman. Just like last time!"

Her voice is so shrill, chills run over me. It's a desperate woman's cry. A last chance. Isn't it?

Jack holds her by the throat. "Shut up, you little bitch. You'll pay for touching Clementine. She's not yours. She's ours."

"Ours?" I say, stepping toward Jack. "What do you mean, ours?"

Jack squeezes Emma's neck, hard.

Harder still.

Hard enough to kill. Emma's gasping, her hands swinging wildly, begging me to help.

I think of the gun in the kitchen drawer. I could go for it, try to stop Jack from killing the woman who hurt the man I love.

"Ledger never deserved you, Penny. He forced himself into your life and never gave you a chance. It's why I did it. Why I did everything. For you. For us. For our life together."

I shake my head, my cancerous blood pulsing in fear. Emma is purple, going limp in his hands. "What do you mean you did everything?"

And then it hits me. Who would think to cut the brakes? Who would know how to alter a truck to make a death look exactly like a suicide? My stomach drops as the horrific truth dawns on me. Pain claws at my heart as I realize just how deep this betrayal has gone.

Jack lets go of Emma, and, lifeless, she falls to the floor. "I killed Ledger, Penny, so we could be together."

CHAPTER 36

We stare at Emma in horror. I clutch my stomach in agony, wondering how my home became a crime scene so quickly. Shock rips through me at what Jack has done — his pre-emptive decision to end Ledger's life. His reckless decision to end Emma's.

One wrong word and he could flip and decide to end mine.

"Don't be scared, Penny. It's going to be okay. I will take care of everything. Take care of you." His eyes plead with me to understand. "I love you, Penny," he says.

I cover my mouth in terror. Scared to say anything that might upset him. Right now, I don't care about setting the facts straight. I just care about getting out of this house in one piece, I care about reuniting with my children and never letting them go again. Ever.

"I always cared about you," he continues, taking my silence as hope. "But ever since the Fourth of July, I knew. I knew you were mine. You and Ledger fought that night, remember? And it killed me to think he didn't treat you the way you deserved."

I look at the gun heavy in his hand, Emma at his feet. If I do or say the wrong thing right now, I might end up just like her.

I can't let that happen. Not when Ledger is gone. Our children need me. Ours. Ledger's and mine. The children we made. Not Emma's. Not Jack's.

Ours.

"You messed with the brakes?" I ask, stepping toward him. My eyes fix on his, but my mind is focused on the gun in his hand. I take his other hand in my own, wanting him to let down his guard.

He nods, stepping closer. Close enough to wrap his hands around my neck and end my life just the same. "I had to. God, I love you, Penny. So damn much. I always have. This was the only way we could be together."

The picture is fuzzy, but I try to focus. Jack, always here for me. Supporting me. Always a phone call away. Here the moment Ledger died, stepping in to fill the void.

"You did that for us?" I lift my chin, lick my lips. This is not the moment to fall apart. Still, tears roll down my face. He sees them as adoration, but my body shakes with disgust. This man standing with me now took away the love of my life. He broke apart my family. But by God, he will not break me.

Jack nods. Setting down the gun on the counter, he takes my face in his hands. Tears streak my cheeks and I tell myself to wait. The cops will be here. Any moment. This will all be over.

I let him kiss me.

The kiss he killed Ledger for. The kiss he killed Emma for. I don't want to give him what he wants. I want something else.

Something worth more than my lips against his, the mouth of a killer. I want to live. I want to fight this cancer. I want to watch my children grow, to become healthy and strong. To see them flourish.

Emma was right. My life is perfect because my children are in it. Children that Ledger gave me. The life we never planned on becoming our dream come true.

Jack kisses me deeply, his body hard against my belly, and it makes me sick. I want to vomit, to shove him back. To make him pay. He kisses me as if thinking this is what love is. Holding me in his arms, trying to kiss away the horror of what he's done.

But that isn't love. Love is so much more than sex. And love doesn't fade over a stupid fight on the Fourth of July. Love is a messy, complicated thing. It is sacrifice, and it is falling apart and learning to get back up. It is holding out a hand and not letting go. Even when it's hard.

Especially when it's hard.

And right now, love is here — even in the midst of this mess, I feel it welling up within me. My love for Ledger is stronger now than it has ever been.

Jack's and my feet crunch against the shattered glass from the family photo as he pushes me toward the wall. Love is a fragile, breakable thing that can only be repaired when two people are willing to hold each shard of glass in their hands, knowing it's sharp enough to cut. When they know it can make them bleed but they decide to fix it anyway.

Ledger lied to me, and I held the pregnancy against him. Angry for so long at what it took from me.

Only later realizing what it gave me.

Courage to believe that love at first sight was real. And it was. He made up a name the night we met, willing a fresh start to begin.

When we met, he knew he couldn't go on living as Henry James. It would kill him. *Emma would kill him.* So he didn't. He started over, he gave me his breakable heart, and I didn't let go. Not once. Not ever.

Jack pulls back. "God, I wanted to do that for so long," he says. Behind him, I see Emma moving, standing. My body convulses, the shock of her being alive coursing through my veins. Jack is so lost in me, in our future, he doesn't hear her.

I swallow, my skin crawling as a killer holds me in his arms. "Was it worth it?" I ask in a whisper. I step back, reaching for a napkin to wipe my tears away, creating much-needed space between us. "I mean, Jack, you could go to jail for this."

He shakes his head, smiling over at me. "No, the cops aren't coming. They'll never know. It's our secret. We'll get the insurance money. We can get rid of Emma. No one even knows who she is. Her only living relative has memory loss. This won't be hard. And Penny, we can start our life together."

"Just like that," I say in a whisper as Emma reaches for the gun. "Was it hard to kill him? Your best friend?"

"I thought it would be easier," he says, his eyes desperate for me to understand. "I fucked with the brakes at the truck stop, and after, I followed behind him in my own car. But then he rolled out, a quarter of a mile before his truck went over. I had to get out of my car." He shakes his head, rubbing his temples.

"What did you do?" I ask, wrapping my hand around his neck, comforting him, my eyes blurry with tears as I draw the man who murdered the love of my life closer.

"I had to kick him over the cliff," he says. "There was no other way."

I can't help it — I heave, curling over. Sick. It's impossible to pretend.

I wipe my mouth as Emma pulls the trigger.

Shooting Jack in the back. Once. Twice. Three times to make sure he is really, truly dead.

She tries to shoot again, and again, but the bullets are gone.

She drops the gun, as if shocked at her own actions.

His head turns. His eyes lift, meeting mine, the gunshots reverberating through the room as he falls.

My body shakes as I spit out the last words he will ever hear. "Fuck you, Jack Barrett."

His eyes roll back, blood on the lips I just forced myself to kiss. And he doesn't say another thing.

But I do.

I take the gun he set on the counter and I lift it to Emma. "There is only one way this is going to end," I tell her.

"Don't," she says. "I told you, I didn't kill him, I—"

"Stop talking," I say, walking toward her with the gun raised, reaching into the junk drawer and pulling out the duct tape.

I always said I was resourceful.

CHAPTER 37

She knows I can kill her. The gun is raised, and I could so easily pull the trigger.

Instead, I call 911, knowing the neighbors must have heard the gunshots. We don't have much time alone. Then I use the duct tape to keep her in place and make her talk.

Starting from the beginning.

Their first part goes like this: They were in college, at Portland State. Henry was lonely, at a big school, in a big city. No family, few friends. Trying hard to get the degree that was free of charge due to a grant for children aging out of the foster care system. Emma grew up taking care of her mom. But her mom was now in a home for early-onset dementia. She needed someone new to take care of.

She chose Henry James.

According to her, it was a once-in-a-lifetime kind of love.

Their daughter, Eva, was born a year later. Eva died of unknown causes when she was only three months old. Emma never recovered. I know this part from before, from the first day we met. Then, it hurt too much to hear. But I can handle it now. Now, I honestly believe I can handle anything.

So I take a deep breath and listen. Because there is no more time to tiptoe around the truth — the police are coming, and we're working with minutes here.

Emma, who now sits taped to a chair in my living room, a dead man on the floor a few feet from us, has a softer viewpoint of her life circumstances than Sheriff Lawson did when he gave me the arrest report.

"I was angry," she says. "My daughter died, and everyone was moving on. And it was wrong of me, but I took my anger out on Henry. He refused to fight back."

"But it wasn't a fight you wanted, was it?" I ask her, gun still raised. "You wanted Eva to be alive."

Emma cries, unable to wipe her tears, and I try so damn hard to see her as a person, not as a monster that drove Ledger to faking his death. "It was my fault," she confesses, choking on her words. Admitting her truth for the first time in her life. "She was in her crib and she . . . she . . . never woke up."

My heart breaks for her then. Not for the woman she became later, when she became dangerous and unhinged . . . but for the woman she was before.

The woman who died the day her baby did.

"She stopped breathing and I called 911, but it was too late. She was gone."

If Eva's death had never happened, would Emma and Henry James have lived happily ever after? Their story would be so different.

And so would mine.

Maybe I would have kept putting my tips in my travel jar and been in Belgrave by now. Maybe I'd have a Europass and a backpack and experiences I could taste and touch.

But I wouldn't have Tiny and Benny. I wouldn't have had Ledger. And this life that I thought was small suddenly seems so incredibly big.

I cry now, listening to her. Because losing Eva changed her, and I can understand that. Because losing Ledger is changing me.

But Emma's grief turned her into something feral and fierce.

Something terrifying and tragic.

I won't let mine make me small.

"He was scared of me. I know that now," she says, shaking as she speaks. "He wasn't sad enough, and it made me mad. Why wasn't he angry the same way I was?"

"How mad?" I need the entirety of her truth. "How angry?"

She blinks, knowing that lying won't save her, won't bring Eva back. It's all over.

"I would hold a knife to his throat while he slept, and I told him I'd do it," she says. "That if he tried to leave me, I'd track him down and make him wish he'd never met me. I became a monster."

I listen, grinding my teeth, knowing that for all her tragedy, she hasn't quite learned anything. She came here today and pointed a gun at my face.

"You tried to take Tiny," I say.

"I'm sorry."

"Are you?" I ask.

She nods. "I killed Jack to prove it. I'm so sorry, Penny. I snapped the day Eva died and I've been in pieces ever since. Then I saw the news story about Henry and I thought . . . maybe . . . maybe finally I'd get some closure. Finally get some peace. But then I met you. You. Perfect Penny with her perfect life, and I got jealous. So jealous of you. Because the love I had with Henry . . ." Her shoulders shake. "It wasn't this. It wasn't like yours. Henry was always lost, but the way you speak of him, it's like he was found."

* * *

Sirens roar close to the house as Emma and I make our peace.

Peace. Crazy to imagine with a woman who made my husband's life a living hell, but love is a powerful thing. It moves mountains, after all.

I stand at the kitchen sink, splashing cold water over my face as I try to think through exactly what I need to say to the officers.

Emma, though, is the one who is prepared to do the talking.

When the police officers rush through the door, Sheriff Lawson is with them. His eyes find mine, and I can finally breathe since Emma showed up at my house and this nightmare began.

It ends now.

Paramedics come in with a stretcher; Jack's body is lifted. He is dead — blood covers him, the kitchen floor — and I cover my mouth, closing my eyes. Seeing the man who betrayed my family dead is a poor consolation prize, and I don't want it.

"I have a confession to make," Emma James says, her voice loud enough to turn every head in the room. She is sitting on a kitchen chair in the middle of the living room, her hands behind her back, duct taped together, her feet taped to the front legs of the chair.

I didn't want to risk her running.

But after almost losing her life, it seems her perspective has shifted.

"I killed Jack Barrett after he tried to strangle me to death, and then he threatened to do the same to Penny."

"And how do you know Penny?"

"I knew her husband, Ledger Stone, a long time ago. I saw his story on the news and decided to connect with her since I knew him."

Sheriff Barrett looks at me. "Is this true?"

I nod.

"And why is she tied up?" he asks, perplexed. "If she just saved your life?"

"Because she asked me to detain her until you arrived."

"It's true," Emma says. "I'm not well. I'm a threat to the public. I am voluntarily asking to be placed in a psychiatric program to be evaluated."

Without fighting it, Emma allows an officer to remove her from the bindings. I watch, tears running down my cheeks as Emma's life changes again, this time in front of my eyes. She is finally going to get the help she needed a long time ago.

Sheriff Lawson asks me to explain what happened with Jack. As I recount the story, he writes everything down. I explain how he messed with the brakes and then followed Ledger, wanting to see the moment his truck went off the road. I tell him what Jack told me, that Ledger rolled out of the truck and that Jack kicked him over.

"Oh my God!" I gasp, piecing Jack's story together as I say it out loud. "Oh, God, I think they've been looking in the wrong spot . . . I think I know where his body is."

CHAPTER 38

Before I get in Sheriff Lawson's cruiser, I walk over to Emma and give her a quick hug. Maybe I'm too soft, but I'm sick and soon I might die, and if I can embrace a woman who is alone in this world, why wouldn't I?

Life is short, I'm learning. We have no idea when we might lose the ones we love the most.

Emma leaves. She's being escorted to the nearest voluntary mental health inpatient unit. I'll take out a permanent restraining order against her, of course. But before the officers arrived, she made me a promise to stay until she was well and to never seek us out. To let us live in peace.

It's a promise she might break, a promise I have no control over.

A promise all the same.

And isn't that all any of us can ask for? Words said in good faith, hoping they are true. Emma may not get the professional help we both know she needs, but God, I hope she does. I don't want her to live the rest of her life carrying the guilt over her daughter's death. That won't help anyone.

She needs to move on, to be set free. And as she rides away in a police car, she looks back, palm pressed to the window, a sadness in her eyes I understand. Sorrow born from loss.

I don't know if she'll find the help she is looking for. But I hope she does before it's too late. Ledger saw a therapist for five years and still never got to the point where he could tell me his whole story, from beginning to end. Is that for lack of love or *because* of his love? I might never know.

Or I might know very, very soon.

"You ready to go, Penny?" Lawson asks.

"One second," I say, walking over to Bethany. She pulled up to the house with her family minutes after the ambulance arrived. She was given a brief rundown, but I need to say goodbye.

"You think he's still alive?" she asks, hope in her eyes.

"No." I shake my head, pull her close. "I just want his body to be recovered, so he can be put to rest. Jack said he rolled out of the truck a quarter mile before it went over. I've been to the accident site. A quarter mile means he would have been pushed over an entirely different portion of the mountain. His body could be there — search and rescue never went to that side."

"Just prepare yourself, Penny. It might be hard to—"

I cut her off. "I know. I know. It's going to be difficult to see him, if his body is found at all. But I need closure. We all do."

The drive seems to last forever. I call Mom, explaining what happened, ending the call quickly. I have no interest in telling the sheriff that my husband faked his own death. And even though Emma never got life insurance money — they never took out policies either — it's still not legal, what he did to escape her.

"There's so much more I need to tell you," I say to my mom as we near the accident site. There is already a search and rescue crew at work, looking on the left side of the mountain. "Until I see you again, just please, please take care of the twins. I miss them so much."

"Are you okay?" she asks. "I wish I was there with you."

"I know, Mom. But what I really need is for the kids to feel safe right now."

When we get to the mile marker, a lane is already closed and there are officers directing traffic. It's late in the day, but the sun is out and I take that as a positive sign. But by the time day turns to night, I start to get anxious.

"Can you please repeat what Jack Barrett said?" a highway patrolman asks, going back over my testimony.

I run a hand through my hair, retelling the story. I'm exhausted, but I'll keep repeating it until Ledger's body is found.

The sky grows dark and stars begin to light up the sky. If he's found, it will be a miracle.

But love at first sight is impossible too, isn't it?

Yet it's real.

The moment I met Ledger, I knew. He was mine and I was his and everything that has happened between that moment and this tells me not to give up hope. Not just yet.

There are so many impossible things in life that, once we experience them, stop seeming so unfathomable. They become miracles. And how many tiny miracles can one person live through?

Too many to count.

When a crew member makes an announcement on a loudspeaker, I start shaking. A blanket is wrapped around my shoulders, and Sheriff Lawson is at my side.

"We found a body," he tells me. "At this moment, a team is on site and beginning to prepare for transport at the roadside level."

Silently, Lawson and I walk to the edge of the gorge, where they found the body. Still not identified as the body of my husband.

But I feel him before I see him. Here. Mine. Like he always was and always will be, till death do us part. Even though he is gone, I realize the vow I took isn't true at all. It's not till we part because I will love Ledger every day of my life.

I took a vow. I made a promise. And maybe my promise means something different than Ledger's promise did, but I can choose which story I want to tell myself.

And right now, in this miracle that isn't so tiny, I am choosing the ending I want.

When his body is lifted to the side of the road, I run.

CHAPTER 39

My feet catch on a rock, and I nearly fall. Lawson has my arm, helping me stand. Tears fill my eyes. I hold my breath, too scared to draw in air.

When I reach him, the rescue workers move aside, and an ambulance blares in the distance. The roar of my pounding heart is louder than the sirens. Ledger is here.

Bloody, broken, eyes closed, lips cracked. Gone.

My hands cradle his face. His eyes are closed and, God, what I would give to have him look into my eyes. Everything. He was my one and only, and he has my heart and I have his, and how is this man who loves so deep, so well, gone?

The paramedics are here and they want to pull me away because anyone looking at this body wouldn't know who it is. They call my name and urge me to move. I won't. Can't.

Ledger is a shell of a man, but he is my man. And I know. I won't leave, even if they ask me to step back, because I just got here.

"Ledger," I whisper, my salty tears falling on his sunburned cheeks, his beard thicker than I remember. I want to run my fingers through it and kiss each inch of him and never, ever let him go. I whisper again. "Ledger."

Leaning down, I kiss his lips. I press my heart to his.

I feel it then.

My world, the one that shifted, changed its axis the day we met at the diner all those nights ago, shifts again.

There is a heartbeat, ever so faint. Ever so strong.

"He's alive," I scream, my voice scratchy and scared, urgent and demanding. "He's alive!"

He's unconscious but breathing. Bleeding, but not all broken. My husband, Ledger Stone, is alive.

The weight of what I've been carrying hits me the moment I feel it, that thump, thump, thump that releases all my doubt. In an instant, all my fears from the past week hit me like a ton of bricks.

He didn't die, didn't kill himself, doesn't have cancer.

But I do.

And now I'm scared in a whole new way.

I reach for his hands even though the medics are pulling me back, but it doesn't matter. The onslaught of emotions takes over and my knees go weak and my vision goes dark and I fall.

* * *

When I wake, I'm in a hospital room, in a mint-green gown. The room is bright white, spotless, and a bouquet of gerbera daisies are on my bedside table.

And there, in the bed next to me, is Ledger.

He's alive. His eyes are on mine. Staring. It's as if he willed me awake.

He's scared.

"What happened to you?" he asks.

I blink, my body weak. Since I got the call he was in an accident, I've been exhausted yet forcing myself to hold it all together. But it's as if my body knew, once Ledger was found, in the flesh, that I could let go.

That when I woke, Ledger would be here to help me stand.

"Last night or since you've been gone?" I ask, my voice rough. Still blindsided by the fact he isn't dead.

"I've been awake for an hour," he says, his voice the balm my broken heart needs. God, I missed him. "Had a visit with Sheriff Lawson and a few other guys on the force." Ledger's face is bruised, like he's been through hell and back. He has. He's in a hospital gown and should probably rest, but he reaches his hand out to me. "I would have died if there hadn't been a rainstorm three nights ago."

Tears fill my eyes. "I drove out there, that day it rained. I drove to the accident site, needing to see it for myself. I screamed at the sky and you know what? The sky cried all the tears I wanted to shed."

I sit up, my feet find the cold linoleum floor. Taking the three steps to Ledger's bed, an IV in my arm, I wheel the bag of fluids with me as I lie in his bed. My heart throbs, the pain of nearly losing him causing the ache.

His left arm is in a cast. He tells me his hip was dislocated, that he cracked four ribs, his left foot was shattered when a rock fell.

But he is alive.

"So," he says, running his calloused palm over my cheek, his pine-green eyes locked with mine. "I know what happened with Jack. With Emma," he says, his voice cracking on her name. "But I need to understand what's happened to you."

"What do you mean?" I ask, tears filling my eyes because he knows. He knows me.

"I mean, why did my girl collapse? You aren't the fainting type, Penny Stone."

"I was exhausted. You were alive. I was scared you weren't."

"What else?"

I look away, because how do you tell the man you'd do anything for that you might not be here in a year?

"Emma tried to kidnap Tiny," I tell him, avoiding the words that will break us both. "You kept so much from me."

Tears splash down Ledger's face, the scar under his eye taking on new meaning. "I wanted to protect you."

"I know."

"Can you forgive me?"

I lace my fingers with his, needing this. Him. "I've been so mad, I thought a thousand things before they found you. That you were with someone else, that you meant for this to happen, that you had cancer, for Christ's sake," I say. "I thought the worst. I prayed for the best. It's been a roller coaster, and you know what I learned?"

"What's that?" He kisses my forehead, and our tears fall and our hearts break for all the things we've thought and all the things we've seen. The things he ran from and the things I told myself.

"I learned that this roller coaster, with you, is one I never want to get off of. I want to ride it all day and all night. Until I can't anymore."

"You're too good for me, Penny Stone."

It's hard to breathe, the tears cascading down my face. "You had a daughter."

He nods. "Losing her changed me. Changed Emma. She would have killed me, wanted me dead, and I may be a hard-ass, but I'd never lay a finger on her. I thought it was for the best, leaving the past behind."

"But you can't, Ledger. You can't just pretend your story never happened. It's yours."

"She knew I wanted to leave and she threatened to kill me, and then I met you and for the first time in my goddamn life, I knew what love was. Unconditional love. The love you had for me made me stronger than I'd ever been before. Strong enough to leave."

"You could have divorced her. You could have told me."

He runs his thumb over my cheek. "Told you, Penny? You were barely twenty years old, a woman who had seen hard shit and knew she wanted more for herself, for her life. How could I tell you that I was married, that my wife was crazy, that I was scared? That I wasn't half the man you believed me to be? You would have walked."

"You don't know that. And it wasn't for you to decide."

He closes his eyes, and I breathe him in. "I know that now. But Penny, five years ago, I wasn't the man I am today. I was a coward who knew you were the best thing to ever happen to me. You were this person who saw me as more. The best version of myself. After the twins were born, I wanted to tell you. I wanted to lay it all out there . . . but I was paralyzed with fear."

"What were you so scared of?"

"That I'd lose you and our children. And I'd already lost so damn much."

I consider this, his reasoning. This reckoning coming five years late. But not too late. I'm alive and he's alive, and we have to fix this.

"You lost your parents. Your foster brother. Your daughter. Your wife. Yourself, Henry James."

He clenches his jaw, tears in his eyes. "Exactly. But then with you, it was like, for the first time in forever, I was found."

"Fear makes us think and say and do crazy things," I tell him. "And I forgive you for your secrets because I get it. I get it now." I run my fingers over his face, closing my eyes, memorizing his skin. "I'm dying," I tell him. Eyes squeezed tight. "I have leukemia."

With the words out, he takes my hand in his hands, and I look at him. This man. My man. My world, the one who has half of my heart, and I'm dying and I don't ever want to say goodbye. I don't want to miss a thing. I want this. A forever with him and the twins, and I'm scared I won't ever get that.

"No," he says, pressing his face to my chest, sobs wracking his body the same way they wrack mine, and I can't die. I can't. I need more of this. His body against my body and his heart against my heart. And I can't die. This whole time he has thought it was him that sick. That was dying. But it was me.

"There was an error with the lab — they mixed up our results. I'm sick. It's probably why I fainted. Why I've been sleeping so much. Why I'm still here in this hospital bed. I have tests today," I say, running my fingers through his thick hair.

"We'll fight it." He pulls me to him, his arms around me, and I cry into his shoulder, the place I belong. "This roller coaster isn't over, Penny Stone. Not now, after we just got through this."

CHAPTER 40

The twins come into the hospital room with my mom, Benjamin and Clementine running to Ledger, arms wide, hair flying, eyes so bright.

"Papa!" they shout, covering him with kisses. Dr. Winters comes into the room behind them. She sets the kids on my bed, and Ledger holds them with his one arm so tight they laugh, but they squeeze him right back, little fingers gripping his right arm, not wanting to let go.

Dr. Winters says Ledger is needed for a final CT scan. Three nurses come in to wheel him out; Ledger protests, but finally he relents when I tell him to. He smiles at me and I smile back, and for the first time since he went missing, I think that just maybe the world is going to be okay.

I want to believe our little world isn't going to break, but I'm confused and exhausted from a week-long adrenaline high, and now that Ledger and I are both here, breathing — I can barely believe it's actually over. I just came to terms with my husband's death, and now he's alive. It's as if we've been given a second chance at life.

But really, this is his third shot. And it isn't going to end the way he hopes. The way any of us hope.

My heart tightens knowing how bittersweet our story is.

"Can we come?" Benny asks, and the nurse says sure. Everyone is overly accommodating for the man who made it out alive. Tiny takes her papa's hand and I watch them go, Mom coming to my bedside, taking my hand in hers.

"Oh, Penny," she sighs. "I can't believe you fainted, but I'm so glad you're okay."

Dr. Winters and I share a look, and I know Mom hasn't heard the news. My doctor excuses herself and tells me she'll be back in a bit to take me for the testing.

"What testing?" Mom asks, confused.

I tell her then, the two of us alone.

Her eyes fill with tears and she covers her mouth. "No, Penny," she says, shaking her head. "It can't be."

I bite my lip, shoulders shaking. "Not what I expected either. But at least now we know. It's not too late to fight this."

"You're so young," she says, cupping my cheek with her hand. "Too young for this."

"Can you try to forgive Ledger?"

Her eyebrows lift, my words not the ones she was expecting. "That's what you want? After all the secrets, you still think—"

"Mom, I hate that this happened, but I love him. It's not because I'm a pushover or weak — it's because it's my story. And this is how I want it to end. I have a choice in that — not everyone does."

"I don't think you're weak." Mom runs her fingertips over her forehead. "It's me who has been weak for so long. Letting men walk all over me." She gives me a sad smile. "I was a bad example. Those guys back in high school, I know they weren't kind to you."

"You think Ledger is like them?"

Mom shakes her head, hard. Eyes set firm. "No. Ledger is not like them." Tears slide down her cheeks. "I think he's a lot like me. Screwed up a hell of a lot and in need of a second chance. You are his second chance. And your babies are mine. You were meant for him, the same way they were meant for me."

211

"Good," I say. "Because you two need to get along; I might not always be here, and you're family."

"Don't say that," Mom says, shaking her head. "Don't, Penny. Believe in a miracle."

"Oh, Mom," I say. "I've always believed in miracles."

* * *

When we get to the house, I'm relieved that it no longer looks like a crime scene. I left it with blood on the floor, sirens in the driveway, Jack on a stretcher.

Still, it no longer feels like home.

I close my eyes, gripping the countertop. The sound of bullets, the look in Jack's eyes — his mouth on mine — it makes me ill. I lean over the sink, sick with memories. Benny gets me a towel, and Ledger hands me a glass of cold water. I move to the couch with Tiny, pulling my little girl into my lap, kissing her hair. I can't stay here long, in this house.

Ledger knows.

We spent three days in the hospital, and I underwent rounds of testing. In the end, lots of decisions were made. They aren't ones I'm happy about, but I doubt any cancer treatment plan brings a smile to someone's face. The kids know — we told them the day after Ledger was found. They wanted to understand why we were still at the hospital.

"I'm sick," I told them. "Really sick. And I need the doctors to help me figure out how I can be healthy again."

"Do you need vitamins?" Benny asked.

I nod. "Yes, lots of vitamins. And medicine, too. But some of the medicine will make me even sicker for a bit before it makes me better."

Tiny started crying. "I don't want you to get sick, Mama."

"I know, baby, I don't want to be sick either. But look at us," I said. "We're all here, together. And just knowing that makes me stronger."

It was hard to try to explain cancer to four-year-olds, but they didn't need details. The most important thing for them to know was that we were stronger together than we were apart.

Now, the kids run outside to play on the swing set, and I drink my glass of water, watching them through the window. I start chemo tomorrow. I'm scared. Ledger sits next to me, and I lie down, my head in his lap, my feet hanging over the arm of the couch. "I got a call from Jack's attorney," I tell him.

Ledger frowns; the reality of his best friend trying to take his life is so horrific, neither of us can really talk about it. "Why did he call?"

"Jack had a will, he had it drawn up last month. He named me as the beneficiary on his life insurance policy."

Ledger shakes his head. "Which means he was planning this, killing me to get to you."

"Scary, right?" I say. Ledger runs his hand through my hair, I look up into his eyes. "I'm taking it. The money."

"You are?"

"The bastard owes me this at least, don't you think?"

Ledger swallows. "It's kind of twisted, though, isn't it?"

"More twisted than you faking your death?" My words sound harsher than I meant. "Ledger — it's a million-dollar policy."

"Shit." Ledger's eyebrows knit together. "I wish I could be the one to give you that. Give you what you deserve."

"What I deserve? What does that even mean?" I sigh, pulling Ledger down to my mouth. "Because, baby, all of this, this life with you, it's all so much more than I ever dreamed."

CHAPTER 41

The stories weren't lying. Paris is beautiful in the spring.

When we planned the trip, it was under heartbreaking circumstances. We thought this would be the last time we could do something so beautiful together.

But life can constantly surprise us, can't it?

Benjamin and Clementine are rolling around the grass in Luxembourg Park, and I sit on a blanket with my husband, drinking chilled white wine and eating cheese and bread and more cheese. More bread. Smiling. Laughing. Holding this all so tight and at the same time letting it all go.

"Where will we vacation next?" I ask my husband.

"I will go wherever you want," Ledger says, reaching for my hand. His hair is longer now. The rugged man I fell in love with has aged this year, as he held my hand while I went through chemo and radiation, a clinical trial.

And then, letting go. Surrendering. Knowing that whatever happened next with me, and this one precious life I have, would be lived to the fullest with the time I had left.

And then, the miracle we had all been hoping for.

The chemo worked.

The cancer is gone.

Life was no longer about being one step closer to the end, each day has become another chance to love as deeply and fully as possible.

It's hard to picture him as a long-haul trucker. But it's hard to imagine me at Over Easy, waiting tables. Both of us wearing the skin we needed to, when we needed to. Now, with the insurance money from Jack, and the settlement we received from the lab, we will never be paycheck to paycheck again.

I feel like I have a new lease on life. I plan to write, to travel, to be the best mom and wife I can possibly be. Ledger is still deciding what sort of work he would love to do, he is thinking about going back to school.

We flew from Argentina to France last week, and he's visibly less stressed than he was when we started this trip. A trip that will last as long as possible now that I am cancer-free.

Mom is here with us. She is walking toward the twins with two gelato-filled waffle cones. She hands them over and they squeal, the three of them walking to the pond to look at the birds gliding over the river.

"I'm so glad she's here," I say, resting my head against Ledger's chest. "Weird that Sheriff Lawson is going to meet up with us in Rome, isn't it?"

Ledger laughs, kissing my neck. "Very weird. But damn, it's pretty sweet. I've never seen your mom so happy. Also, I think we can start calling him Lawson now, not Sheriff."

"Agreed." I smile. "And Bethany and the kids are already on the plane. They'll be here in the morning."

"The twins are gonna freak over Disney Paris."

"Bethany says Thomas hasn't stopped talking about meeting Buzz Lightyear since he found out about the trip."

I lie in his lap, closing my eyes, listening to the sounds of people around us, laughing and talking in a different language, living life. Ledger's fingers run through my hair and I rest, lost in memories. When Benny and Tiny run over to the blanket, my eyes blink open, the sun shining behind them, the blue skies up ahead. Strawberry ice cream on their lips and giggles escaping their mouths. I pull them to me, and they know what I need right now is this: my children pressed to my heart.

Bethany told me to write my own ending; Jack did too. Neither of them mentioned the middle. Or really, the third act.

That part is tricky, because that's the part where things so often fall to pieces.

But this right here? This isn't falling apart.

This is my life coming together.

My ending — the one I've been working towards my entire life — I have it.

THE END

THE JOFFE BOOKS STORY

We began in 2014 when Jasper agreed to publish his mum's much-rejected romance novel and it became a bestseller.

Since then we've grown into the largest independent publisher in the UK. We're extremely proud to publish some of the very best writers in the world, including Joy Ellis, Faith Martin, Caro Ramsay, Helen Forrester, Simon Brett and Robert Goddard. Everyone at Joffe Books loves reading and we never forget that it all begins with the magic of an author telling a story.

We are proud to publish talented first-time authors, as well as established writers whose books we love introducing to a new generation of readers.

We have been shortlisted for Independent Publisher of the Year at the British Book Awards three times, in 2020, 2021 and 2022, and for the Diversity and Inclusivity Award at the Independent Publishing Awards in 2022.

We built this company with your help, and we love to hear from you, so please email us about absolutely anything bookish at feedback@joffebooks.com

If you want to receive free books every Friday and hear about all our new releases, join our mailing list: www.joffebooks.com/contact

And when you tell your friends about us, just remember: it's pronounced Joffe as in coffee or toffee!

ALSO BY ANYA MORA

STANDALONES
MY HUSBAND'S WIFE